Christmas is my favorite time of year! This year, I got an early Christmas present from my family—horseback-riding lessons. I was so excited!

But on my first day at the stables, things started to go wrong. First I found out that all the other girls in my beginners' class were elementary-school kids. *Then* I ran into Hannah, a really popular girl from school—and she thought I was taking an intermediate class. I was so embarrassed about being in the baby class that I didn't tell Hannah the truth.

Now there's a big Christmas horse show coming up. Hannah expects me to be in the intermediate class—and she's invited everyone from school to come watch. They're all going to see me humiliated. Even worse, Hannah will think I lied to her. It's a mess!

But there is one thing about this Christmas that *isn't* a mess: my family.

Right now there are nine people and a dog living in our house—and for all I know, someone new could move in at any time. There's me, my big sister, D.J., my little sister, Michelle, and my dad, Danny. But that's just the beginning.

When my mom died, Dad needed help. So he asked his old college buddy, Joey Gladstone, and my

Uncle Jesse to come live with us, to help take care of me and my sisters.

Back then, Uncle Jesse didn't know much about taking care of three little girls. He was more into rock 'n' roll. Joey didn't know anything about kids, either—but it sure was funny watching him learn!

Having Uncle Jesse and Joey around was like having three dads instead of one! But then something even better happened—Uncle Jesse fell in love. He married Rebecca Donaldson, Dad's co-host on his TV show, *Wake Up, San Francisco*. Aunt Becky's so nice—she's more like a big sister than an aunt.

Next Uncle Jesse and Aunt Becky had twin baby boys. Their names are Nicky and Alex, and they are adorable!

I love being part of a big family. Still, things can get pretty crazy when you live in such a full house!

FULL HOUSE™: Stephanie novels

Phone Call from a Flamingo
The Boy-Oh-Boy Next Door
Twin Troubles
Hip Hop Till You Drop
Here Comes the Brand-New Me
The Secret's Out
Daddy's Not-So-Little Girl
P.S. Friends Forever
Getting Even with the Flamingoes
The Dude of My Dreams
Back-to-School Cool
Picture Me Famous
Two-for-One Christmas Fun
The Big Fix-up Mix-up
Ten Ways to Wreck a Date
Wish Upon a VCR
Doubles or Nothing
Sugar and Spice Advice
Never Trust a Flamingo
The Truth About Boys
Crazy About the Future
My Secret Secret Admirer
Blue Ribbon Christmas

Club Stephanie:

#1 Fun, Sun, and Flamingoes
#2 Fireworks and Flamingoes
#3 Flamingo Revenge

Available from MINSTREL Books

FULL HOUSE™
Stephanie

Blue Ribbon Christmas

Emily Costello

A Parachute Press Book

READING

A MINSTREL® BOOK

Published by POCKET BOOKS
New York   London   Toronto   Sydney   Tokyo   Singapore

A MINSTREL PAPERBACK *Original*

A Minstrel Book published by
POCKET BOOKS, a division of Simon & Schuster Inc.
1230 Avenue of the Americas, New York, NY 10020

A PARACHUTE PRESS BOOK

ISBN: 0-671-00830-7

First Minstrel Books printing November 1997

10 9 8 7 6 5 4 3 2 1

A MINSTREL BOOK and colophon are registered trademarks of Simon & Schuster Inc.

Cover photo by Schultz Photography

Printed in the U.S.A.

Blue Ribbon Christmas

CHAPTER
1

◆ ◀ ◆ ◆

"I found the Christmas decorations!" Stephanie Tanner announced.

"Great!" Darcy Powell said. "Let's get them downstairs before all the cookies disappear!"

Allie Taylor giggled. "Darcy, every Christmas you turn into a cookie monster."

Stephanie and her two best friends were searching the Tanners' tidy attic. Every year Allie and Darcy came over to help decorate the Christmas tree—and to pig out on homemade cookies and hot chocolate. It was a tradition Stephanie and Allie had started in kindergarten, right after they met. When Darcy moved to San Francisco three years ago, she joined in.

"I can't help having a big appetite," Darcy said. "I love Christmas goodies."

"I love Christmas, *period*," Stephanie said.

"Maybe that's because your family already gave you an amazing present," Darcy said. "Even though Christmas is still weeks away!"

"Maybe," Stephanie agreed. "I can't wait to get back in the saddle!"

That morning Stephanie's aunt Becky and uncle Jesse had surprised her with an early Christmas present: six weeks of horseback riding lessons at the Golden Gate Riding Academy. She would have a class every Tuesday, Thursday, and Saturday afternoon.

Stephanie thought it was the best Christmas present she'd ever gotten. Ever since the Tanners had visited a dude ranch two years before, she had been dying to ride again.

"I *have* missed riding," Stephanie went on.

"And don't forget, now you and I get to go to the park together," Allie reminded her. Allie had been taking in-line skating lessons at Golden Gate Park for the past month. She and Stephanie had already agreed to take the bus to their lessons together. Their parents would take turns picking them up.

"Oomph," Allie groaned as she slid a big cardboard box off an attic shelf. "This weighs a ton. What's in here, anyway?"

"I don't know. Tinsel, glass balls—the usual stuff, I guess." Stephanie handed a box to Darcy

2

and picked up a box herself. Then she and her friends clomped down the attic stairs. Stephanie's Christmas spirit soared when they entered the living room. Christmas music played on the stereo. Her entire family was gathered in front of the tree.

"This is so cozy," Stephanie said. "I love the holidays!"

Stephanie's father, Danny Tanner, smiled at her as he carried a tray in from the kitchen. It was loaded with steaming mugs of hot chocolate. D.J., Stephanie's eighteen-year-old sister, followed Danny. She grasped a plate of Christmas cookies.

Aunt Becky sat on the floor with Stephanie's four-year-old cousins, Nicky and Alex. The boys were helping Becky thread pieces of popcorn onto a string.

Michelle, Stephanie's ten-year-old sister, leaned over and helped herself to a handful of popcorn.

"Michelle, stop eating the decorations!" Nicky protested.

"Yeah—leave some for me," Uncle Jesse cried. He knelt under the tree, tightening the screws on the Christmas tree stand.

"That tree is leaning to one side." Joey Gladstone grabbed a cookie and popped it into his mouth. Joey was an old college friend of Danny's. He was also a professional comedian. He'd moved in with the Tanners after Stephanie's mother died.

Jesse crawled out from under the tree. "I can't help it if the tree is crooked. It *grew* that way."

"I think it looks pretty, Daddy," Alex said.

"Thanks, kiddo," Jesse replied.

"Let the decorating begin!" Stephanie said. Darcy and Allie opened their cardboard boxes and started to pull out ornaments. Stephanie plopped down on the floor in front of the tree and opened her own box. "Hey—this isn't Christmas stuff!" she exclaimed.

"What is it?" Danny asked.

"Newspapers," Stephanie replied in surprise. "And some old photographs. And ribbons. Lots of blue ribbons—the kind you win in horse shows."

Becky glanced over Stephanie's shoulder. "Oh, wow! That's my stuff. From when I was riding. I've been meaning to put it into a scrapbook."

"What a great idea! Maybe I'll start a riding scrapbook, too," Stephanie said. "Since I'm taking horseback lessons now."

"Only *you* don't have any ribbons," Michelle pointed out.

Stephanie made a face at her little sister. "Not yet," she said. *But I'm sure I'll have plenty soon*, she added to herself.

Danny knelt down next to Stephanie and peered into the box. "I'd forgotten you were such a good rider, Becky."

"Are you kidding? She was *famous*," Jesse said. "She won a gold medal in a statewide competition."

"Awesome!" Darcy said.

"What did you get the medal for?" Allie asked. She pushed a strand of reddish-brown hair behind her ear.

"Show jumping," Becky replied. "That's a formal type of riding where you jump your horse over fences and gates."

"A gold medal," Darcy repeated. "You must have practiced *so* hard."

Becky laughed. "Not that hard. At least it didn't seem that way to me. I loved to jump—it's like flying. When it goes right, you and the horse are thinking the same thoughts."

"Something like—oats, give me more oats!" Joey joked.

Everyone giggled. Everyone except Stephanie.

She was too busy imagining herself on a sleek horse, trotting around a riding ring as she had at the dude ranch. Then she pictured herself aiming the horse at a four-foot-high fence. How would it feel to fly through the air on a beautiful horse?

It would feel great, Stephanie thought. She closed her eyes and imagined herself clearing a series of high jumps. A crowd chanted *Steph-an-ie! Steph-an-ie!* Stephanie pulled her horse to a stop.

A group of ultracool girls immediately surrounded her. Her riding class! The girls gave her hugs and high-fives. They were all her friends—even though Stephanie won every competition she entered.

"You're the best jumper in the whole state, Stephanie," one of the girls cried. "I can't wait to see you in the Olympics!"

"I can't wait either," Stephanie mumbled.

"Wait for what?" Allie demanded, breaking into Stephanie's thoughts.

"Um, I can't wait to start my riding lessons," Stephanie said. "I've just decided that I'm going to learn how to be a show jumper. Maybe I'll even win blue ribbons—just like Becky!"

"Well, before you do that, can we decorate the tree?" Danny asked.

Stephanie laughed. She, Darcy, and Allie jumped up to string the colorful Christmas lights. An hour later the tree was covered with ornaments and tinsel, and everyone was stuffed from eating cookies.

Darcy and Allie headed home to tackle their homework. Becky and Jesse led the twins up to bed. Stephanie sat on the couch with D.J. and Michelle and together they admired the Christmas tree.

Just then Jesse tiptoed back into the living room. "Did you tell them the secret?" he asked Danny in a loud whisper.

"Secret?" Michelle's eyes lit up. "What secret?"

"Well, Becky's birthday is in a few weeks,"

Danny reminded D.J., Michelle, and Stephanie. "And Joey, Jesse, and I thought it would be fun to throw a surprise party for her."

"Great idea!" D.J. said.

"It's going to be two weeks from Saturday," Jesse added. "We'll tell Becky it's a Christmas party, but then we'll surprise her by turning it into a birthday bash!"

"Sounds like fun." Stephanie grinned. "What can we do to help?"

"Let's see . . ." Danny said thoughtfully.

"I want to get a present for Becky," Michelle announced. "What should I get her, Uncle Jesse?"

Jesse sighed. "Good question. I don't even know what *I'm* going to give her yet."

"Steph, why don't you take Michelle to the mall and help her find a gift?" Danny suggested. "That would be a big help."

"No problem!" Stephanie wanted to get a present for Becky, too—a terrific present. Becky deserved it.

After all, if it wasn't for Becky, Stephanie wouldn't be on her way to being an Olympic show jumper!

CHAPTER
2

◆ ◄ ◆ ◆

"Show-jumping history, here I come," Stephanie announced on Saturday morning. She and Allie bounded off the bus at Golden Gate Park.

"I'll come back to the stables as soon as my skating lesson is over," Allie told her.

"Great," Stephanie said. "That way you can watch the end of my lesson. Maybe you'll even get to see me jump."

Allie shook her head. "Steph, I don't think you can be a show jumper after one lesson," she teased.

Stephanie grinned. "Come on, how hard could it be?"

"Well, it took me four lessons before I knew how to stop on my Rollerblades," Allie pointed out. "And I didn't have to teach a horse how to do it with me!"

"Okay, so I won't learn to jump today." Stephanie shrugged. "But I can introduce you to the girls in my riding class. I can't wait to see who they are. Maybe there will be some kids from school."

She glanced at her watch. "Yikes! My first class starts in ten minutes!" She felt a jolt of excitement.

"Later!" Allie gave Stephanie a wave and ran off.

"Bye," Stephanie called. She turned and rushed through the arched gateway that led to the Golden Gate Riding Academy.

Inside she saw a long, low building. *That must be the horses' new stable*, she thought. Stephanie hadn't been to the academy in a year or two, and she was surprised to see how much had changed. In front of the stable stood a fenced-off riding ring. She could see another ring farther away, behind the stables. And past that lay a huge pasture, where a few horses were grazing.

Stephanie glanced around, looking for someone who might be in her class and know where to go. But all she saw were a couple of little girls.

I guess I'll just have to find my way on my own, Stephanie thought. She spotted a tiny building that was painted green and white. A carved wooden sign above the door read OFFICE. Stephanie hurried inside.

A guy about D.J.'s age sat behind the wooden counter. He had longish blond hair tucked under a baseball cap, and he wore a plaid shirt and grubby jeans.

"Can I help you?" the guy asked.

"I'm starting beginning dressage today," Stephanie told him. Becky had explained to Stephanie that dressage was a formal type of riding—good basic training for horses *and* riders.

"Name?" the guy asked, picking up a clipboard.

"Stephanie Tanner."

"Okay, you're on the list." He pushed his cap back and smiled at her. "You can leave your stuff in the locker room behind the office. Then go straight to the stables. Your teacher's name is Cora. Oh, and I'm Clint. I'm a junior instructor here. Just let me know if you have any questions."

"Thanks, Clint," Stephanie said. She turned toward the locker room door.

"Oh, one more thing," Clint called. "Here's your riding helmet. You have to wear it at all times. Just bring it back here at the end of your class."

Stephanie took the round helmet. Then she rushed into the locker room. Her class would begin in five minutes, and she definitely didn't want to be late.

Stephanie quickly pulled off her school clothes and slipped into her oldest pair of jeans, a beat-up sweatshirt, and a pair of riding boots. She stuffed her backpack into a tall locker and slammed the door closed. Then she rushed over to the stables.

Where's my class? Stephanie wondered. All she saw was a group of little girls gathered around a petite woman with spiky black hair. *I hope I'm in the right place,* Stephanie thought. *Maybe I should ask.*

She made her way through the group of younger girls and hurried up to the instructor. "Excuse me," Stephanie said. "Could you tell me where to find Cora's class?"

"This is it," the woman answered. "I'm Cora. What's your name?"

"Stephanie Tanner," Stephanie said. "But . . . this can't be my class."

"What class are you in?" Cora prompted her.

"Um, I'm supposed to be in beginning dressage," Stephanie explained.

Cora nodded. "This is beginning dressage. We'll be starting in just a minute." She turned to talk to one of the other students.

Stephanie glanced around. Not one of the other girls looked older than twelve!

"Excuse me?" Stephanie tapped Cora's shoulder. "Um, are you sure this is the right class? I think somebody made a mistake."

"Is something wrong?" Cora asked.

Yes! Stephanie thought. *I don't belong in this class! These kids are all Michelle's age!*

"Well, I just thought there might be a class . . .

11

I mean, I expected to be with . . . older kids," she said.

"Sorry," Cora told her with a smile. "This is the only beginning dressage class at the stables. Usually we have older people in the class, but this group turned out to be pretty young."

"Oh," Stephanie said. "Okay."

"Let's get started," Cora called. "First of all, I need to get an idea of how much riding you've all done. Who here has ridden before?"

Stephanie's hand shot up. *Maybe if I tell Cora how much riding I've done, she'll move me up to an intermediate class,* she thought.

A couple of the other girls raised their hands, too.

Cora pointed to a redhead with pigtails. "When have you been riding before, Janie?"

"My mom took me on a pony ride for my tenth birthday," Janie announced.

Stephanie's jaw dropped. *Janie is only ten?* she thought in horror. *And she knows nothing about riding? This is worse than I thought.*

"How about you, Stephanie?" Cora asked.

Stephanie snapped her attention back to Cora. "I spent a week on a dude ranch," she said. "I rode for hours and hours every day." *Now Cora will realize I'm way too experienced for this class,* she told herself.

12

"When were you at the dude ranch?" Cora asked.

"Two years ago," Stephanie said.

"Then I think you'll still learn a lot in this class," Cora said. "Let's begin."

"But . . ." Stephanie felt the blood rush to her face. How could she be stuck in a class with a bunch of babies? It was so embarrassing!

"We're going to start by learning how to saddle a horse," Cora announced. "First we take the horse out of his box."

Janie giggled. "Why is he in a box?" she asked. "Was he a present?"

"No—a box is where the horse lives," Cora explained. "It's like a stall, only bigger." She opened the door of the box behind her and led out a beautiful horse with a white streak on his nose. His shiny black coat gleamed in the afternoon sunlight. His dark eyes looked calm and intelligent.

Stephanie gasped. He was the most beautiful horse she had ever seen. She stepped closer to Cora and the horse. "What's his name?" Stephanie asked.

"This is Thunderbolt," Cora replied. "Stephanie, why don't you hold him for a minute?" She handed Stephanie the reins.

Thunderbolt gave a low whinny and tossed his head. Stephanie reached up to stroke his velvety-soft nose. "Good boy," she whispered. "I hope I get to ride you during class." The horse pushed his muzzle against her hand, and Stephanie giggled.

Cora picked up a saddle that had been hanging on the door of Thunderbolt's box. "Who knows what this is?"

"A saddle!" the other girls chorused.

"Right," Cora said. "This is an English saddle, which is perfect for dressage. Notice how deep it is. That allows you to get close to the horse's back and have more control."

Stephanie examined the saddle carefully. She'd never ridden with an English saddle before. The dude ranch had used Western saddles.

After she finished talking about the saddle, Cora told the class about the bridle and the reins. She even told them what kind of boots they should wear. And she helped them all adjust their riding helmets so that they fit well.

These little kids sure ask a lot of questions. Easy questions, Stephanie thought. Questions she already knew the answers to.

"What's the difference between walking and trotting?" a girl named Lily asked.

"A horse has several different paces," Cora explained. "Walk, trot, gallop, and canter. Walking is the slowest."

No kidding, Stephanie thought. *I thought everyone knew that.*

Finally Cora told all the girls to head out to the

riding ring. Stephanie hurried over to talk to her alone.

"Um, Cora, can I ask you something?"

"Sure," Cora said. "What's up?"

"Are you going to teach us how to jump in this class?" Stephanie asked. "That's what I really want to learn."

"Jumping *is* a lot of fun," Cora agreed. "But we don't teach it in beginning dressage."

"Not at all?" Stephanie frowned. "Well, then maybe I should take another class."

Cora nodded. "We have new classes starting in about ten weeks. You could sign up for jumping then, Stephanie."

"Well, I really want to learn jumping *now*," Stephanie admitted. "Could I switch classes?"

"Sorry—you can't," Cora told her. "We require all our students to take beginning dressage before they take any other class."

"Oh." Stephanie frowned. "How come?"

"Because it's important to learn the basics of riding," Cora explained. "And we want to be sure all our riders know what they're doing before we let them try anything advanced on one of our horses—like jumping. But after you finish this class, you can sign up for jumping next term."

"But I already know a lot of the basics," Stephanie blurted out. "I learned them all at the dude ranch."

Cora smiled at her. "You may be more advanced than the other girls in your class. But that doesn't mean we can change the stable rules for you. You'll have to stay in the beginning dressage class for now."

Stephanie sighed. "Okay," she said.

"Hey, don't be discouraged," Cora told her. "Tell you what—as soon as I think you're ready for a jumping class, I'll let you know. Maybe we can make an exception and let you move up early."

"Thanks, Cora!" Stephanie said.

"Sure thing," Cora replied.

Stephanie smiled as Cora walked to the front of the class. *This is great*, she thought. *Cora just wants to make sure I know how to ride before she moves me up to a jumping class. I bet I'll be a show jumper in no time!*

CHAPTER
3

♦ ◀ ◆ ◆

"Hey, Steph!" Allie rushed into the locker room. "How was your first class?"

Stephanie made a face. "Terrible!"

"What?" Allie cried. "How come?"

Stephanie lowered her voice. "All of the girls are Michelle's age. And the instructor is treating us all like we're five-year-olds! She actually taught us what a saddle was."

Allie shook her head sympathetically. "That stinks," she said. "But wasn't it fun at all?"

"Well, there were some good parts," Stephanie admitted. "The instructor is really nice—it's not her fault the other kids are babies."

Stephanie picked up her backpack and led the way out of the locker room.

"Oh, and she assigned me to the most perfect

horse," she went on. "His name is Thunderbolt, and he's beautiful. And we're going to be riding English saddles, which are totally elegant."

"Well, it doesn't sound *that* bad. You like your horse," Allie pointed out. "That's the most important thing."

Stephanie shrugged. "I guess. But I'd like him better if I were jumping him."

Allie pushed open the wooden stable door and stepped out into the sunshine. "My mom won't be here to pick us up for another ten minutes," she said.

"That's okay," Stephanie answered. "We can watch some of the other riders until she gets here."

Stephanie led the way over to the riding ring and leaned up against the fence. On the other side of the ring, a girl sat on a tall brown horse. His chestnut coat gleamed and he had a white sock above each hoof.

"What a beautiful horse," Stephanie exclaimed. He pranced about as the girl's instructor set up some fences around the ring.

"Look—she's going to jump!" Stephanie told Allie. "Oh, I am so totally jealous!"

"You are?" Allie asked. "Look at the height of those fences. I wouldn't want to jump over them. They're almost as tall as we are!"

"Shhh!" Stephanie cried. "There she goes!" They watched as the girl urged her horse into a gallop and headed straight for the first fence. Stephanie held her breath as the chestnut horse smoothly cleared the first jump. The rider bent her knees and lifted her body above the horse's back. She gracefully absorbed the shock as the horse hit the ground. Without pausing, the horse continued on to the second and third jumps.

"Wow, she's good," Stephanie said. "She made those jumps look like no big deal. And her form was perfect!"

The rider turned her horse around. Stephanie saw a triumphant grin spread over her face.

Stephanie smiled back. She could just imagine how it felt to take those three jumps so smoothly. No wonder the girl seemed happy.

Suddenly Allie grabbed Stephanie's arm. "Hey! That's Hannah Marsh!" she exclaimed.

Stephanie squinted at the rider's face. "You're right!" she said. "I didn't recognize her with her hair up in the riding helmet."

Hannah was another ninth grader at John Muir Middle School. She had thick black hair that she usually wore hanging straight down her back.

Hannah was popular at school, but Stephanie didn't know her very well. They had been in the same earth science class in eighth grade.

"I like Hannah," Allie said. "I think she's really sweet."

Stephanie nodded. "I like her, too—especially now that I know she's into horses!"

Hannah had spotted Stephanie and Allie. She waved, then slowed her horse and trotted over to them. Meanwhile, her instructor started to set the jumps even higher.

"Hi!" Stephanie called.

"Hi," Hannah said with a smile. "What are you guys doing here?"

"I'm taking lessons," Stephanie told her. "Today was my first class."

Hannah's blue eyes lit up. "That's so great!" she said. "I didn't know anyone else from John Muir rode at this stable."

"Well, I'm not as good as you," Stephanie admitted. Suddenly she felt a little embarrassed. Hannah was an amazing jumper. She probably thought beginning dressage was for babies.

"Yeah, you're amazing!" Allie told Hannah. "I can't believe you got over those mega-jumps."

Hannah laughed. "Well, Ripley and I are a good team." She patted the horse's neck.

"Is he yours?" Stephanie asked.

"He sure is!" Hannah leaned forward and kissed her horse between the ears. Ripley calmly swished his tail back and forth.

"Wow! It must be cool to have your own horse," Stephanie said. "You're so lucky."

Hannah grinned. "I begged my parents for years,

and they finally gave in. But I used to ride a pretty great horse here at the stables before I got Ripley."

"Which horse?" Stephanie asked.

"Thunderbolt," Hannah said. "He's the most gorgeous horse at the riding academy."

"Hey, Thunderbolt is *my* horse!" Stephanie exclaimed. "I love him."

Hannah nodded. "He's a good jumper, too. I learned to jump on Thunderbolt. I'm glad he's got a new rider who loves him as much as I did."

"So I guess you take private lessons, huh?" Stephanie asked.

"Yeah, usually in the morning before school," Hannah said. "But I had the flu last week. So I'm making up lessons in the afternoons for a few days. What class are you in, Stephanie? Are you taking Cora's class?"

"Um, yeah," Stephanie admitted. *I guess Hannah can tell I'm a beginner*, she thought.

"Good for you. I loved that class," Hannah said.

Stephanie's mouth dropped open. "Really?"

Hannah is just being polite, she thought. *She probably took the beginners' class ten years ago!*

"Sure. Don't you like it?" Hannah asked.

"It's okay, I guess. It just moves a little slowly for me."

"Wow," Hannah said. "Have you done a lot of riding before?"

"More than the rest of the kids in the class,"

Stephanie replied. *Which isn't saying much,* she added to herself.

"Where did you learn to ride?" Hannah asked.

"On vacation," Stephanie explained. "My family went to a dude ranch for a week."

"Well, it's too bad you don't like the class more," Hannah said. "But at least you get to jump."

Allie shot Stephanie a surprised look.

"Jump?" Stephanie repeated.

"Yeah," Hannah said. "In fact, that's when I really fell in love with jumping."

Stephanie stared at Hannah in confusion. "Um, *when* did you fall in love with jumping?" she asked.

Hannah shrugged. "When I took the intermediate class a few years ago."

Intermediate class? Stephanie thought. *What intermediate class?*

"Cora taught me so much," Hannah went on. "She really pushes her students. If you're bored in her class, Stephanie, she'll probably move you on to harder jumps. I bet you'll be taking expert jumps in no time."

"Expert jumps?" Stephanie frowned in confusion. "I doubt it. I mean, Cora said she might move me up ahead of the rest of my class. But I don't think she was talking about letting me take expert jumps."

"Don't worry. It might seem slow at first. But it

will get better. Believe me—Intermediate Jumping was my favorite class," Hannah said.

Stephanie felt her cheeks get hot. Now she understood—Hannah wasn't talking about her beginning class. Hannah thought she was in a more advanced class—not in the baby class.

"Uh, listen, Hannah . . ." Stephanie began to say.

"Hey, are you guys waiting for a ride?" Hannah interrupted. "Because that woman is waving at you."

Allie glanced toward the street. "That's my mom," she said. "We'd better go!"

Stephanie glanced at Hannah. "I actually just started taking Cora's—" she tried to explain.

"Hannah!"

Hannah glanced over her shoulder. "My instructor is calling me," she told Stephanie. "I have to go, too. See you in school!" Hannah turned Ripley back into the ring.

Stephanie followed Allie toward her car. "Steph, does Hannah think you're in the intermediate jumping class?" Allie asked as they walked.

"I guess so." Stephanie shrugged. "I didn't know Cora teaches two different classes. I guess I should tell Hannah that I'm only a beginner. I don't want her to think I was lying or anything."

Allie nodded. "Just explain to her on Monday. No problem."

"Yeah," Stephanie said. "No problem. Except that I wish I really *was* a show jumper like she is!"

Allie laughed as they climbed into the car and said hello to Allie's mom.

Stephanie sighed as they pulled away from the stable.

"Are you okay?" Allie asked.

Stephanie nodded. "I'm just disappointed. I thought I'd make a lot of friends in class. But it feels more like baby-sitting than making friends."

"Bummer," Allie agreed. "Do you think you might quit?"

"No way!" Stephanie cried. "I'm going to be a star jumper like Hannah. And I don't care how many baby classes I have to take to do it!"

CHAPTER
4

◆ ◀ ◣ ◆

"I'm going to get this for Becky's birthday. Isn't it great?" Michelle held up a glittery Barbie doll dress so that Stephanie, Allie, and Darcy could see it.

Darcy's dark eyes widened in surprise. "Becky still plays with Barbies?"

Stephanie rolled her eyes. She had brought Michelle to the mall on Sunday afternoon to shop for Becky's present. Allie and Darcy came along to do some Christmas shopping.

"Michelle, have you ever seen Becky with a Barbie doll?" Stephanie asked.

"I guess not." Michelle reluctantly put the dress back on the shelf. "But it was so pretty."

The four girls wandered out of the toy store and into the crowded mall. Right away Michelle grabbed Stephanie's arm and pulled her toward a sporting goods store.

"Come on, you guys," Michelle urged the others. "Let's go in here!"

"Sounds good to me," Darcy agreed. She loved all kinds of sports—and she was good at most of them.

"Does Becky like to work out?" Allie asked as she followed them in. "You could get her a leotard. Or some socks."

"Socks?" Michelle made a face. "No way!"

"I'm with Michelle," Darcy said. "Socks are much too boring for a present."

"Socks don't have to be boring." Allie pulled up her white jeans so that the others could see her red and white checked socks.

Stephanie and Darcy laughed.

"Those are cool," Michelle said. "But I want to get Becky something. . . ." Her gaze moved over the racks of workout clothes, athletic shoes, and hand weights—and stopped on a display near the wall. "Something like *that!*"

Michelle ran across the carpeted floor and snatched up a neon yellow and orange soccer ball.

Stephanie sighed as she followed Michelle across the store. "When was the last time you saw Becky play soccer?" she asked Michelle.

Michelle shrugged. "Never. But she could learn."

Stephanie took the soccer ball out of Michelle's hands and put it back in the display. "Do you really think she wants to?"

Michelle made a face. "I guess not."

"Well, we know Becky likes to read," Allie put in. "Maybe we can find something for her in the bookstore."

The four girls crossed the mall to Book Street. Michelle immediately headed for a bargain bin in the back. Stephanie wandered toward the riding books. She was looking at a glossy book of horse photographs when Michelle came running up to her.

"I found the perfect present for Becky!" Michelle announced.

Stephanie glanced up from her book. "What?"

"Marauders of Midnight!" Michelle answered.

Allie looked up from the paperback she was reading. "Marauders of Midnight? That sounds like a stupid video game."

Michelle's face fell. "It *is* a video game," she admitted. "But not a stupid one."

Stephanie bit her lip. But she couldn't keep back her laughter. "Michelle, isn't Marauders of Midnight the game you've been bugging Dad to get you?"

Michelle nodded. "It's so much fun. I'm sure Becky would want to play it with me."

"Good try—but Becky never plays video games," Stephanie pointed out.

Michelle slumped against the bookcase. "Finding a good present for Becky is so hard."

"It wouldn't be hard if you thought about what *Becky* likes," Stephanie said. "Not what *you* like."

"But I'm the one buying the present," Michelle complained.

"I know, Michelle," Stephanie told her. "But the idea is to make Becky happy. So you have to look for a gift that *she* wants—even if it's something you would never buy for yourself."

Michelle frowned. "Oh, okay," she muttered. "But it's no fun shopping for something you don't like."

Allie shot Stephanie an amused look. "What are *you* going to get Becky, Steph?" she asked as they headed out of the store.

"I don't know. But it's got to be something great." Stephanie shrugged. "I have plenty of time before the party."

"Stephanie! Over here!"

Stephanie glanced around the cafeteria on Monday afternoon, trying to figure out who was calling her. Finally she spotted Hannah waving from a table near the windows.

"Hannah, hi," Stephanie called. She glanced over at the table where she usually ate lunch. Darcy was already sitting there, eating a sandwich. Anna Rice sat next to her, and Allie sat across from them. Stephanie held up one finger, signaling her friends that she would be over in a minute. Then she fought her way through the crowded cafeteria toward Hannah.

"Hey!" Hannah gave Stephanie a wide smile. She pushed her dark hair behind her ear. "Hailey and Nicole are in the milk line, but they'll be back soon. Do you want to sit with us?"

"Actually, I can stay for only a minute." Stephanie perched on the edge of a chair. "My friends are waiting."

"Okay," Hannah said. "I just wanted to ask you more about Thunderbolt. I haven't spent any time with him since I got Ripley."

"Thunderbolt is so amazing," Stephanie exclaimed. "I mean, I've had only the one class with him so far, but he's a really incredible horse!"

Hannah's eyes sparkled. "I know—his gait is so smooth. And he just loves to jump. I love how excited he gets when he sees a fence in front of him."

Oops! Stephanie thought. *I forgot—Hannah thinks I'm in a jumping class. I guess I'd better set her straight.* She felt a little strange telling Hannah about her baby class in the middle of the lunchroom, though. Hannah probably didn't even remember much about their conversation at the stables.

"Speaking of jumping, I wanted to tell you something," Stephanie began to say. "We were talking about Cora's class the other day . . ."

"Sure." Hannah unwrapped her sandwich. "Are you still bored in it?"

"Well, yeah," Stephanie said. "But that's not—"

"Hi, Stephanie!" Nicole Harwood slipped her tray onto the table and sat down.

"Hey, Nicole!" Stephanie forced herself to smile. *Great*, she thought. *Now I'll have to admit that I'm in the baby class in front of Nicole.*

Nicole was Hannah's best friend. Stephanie had always admired her sense of style. That day Nicole wore a suede jacket over a lime-green dress, and matching lime-green earrings.

"Hannah told me you're taking riding lessons," Nicole said. "Are you as nuts about jumping as she is?"

"Um—" Stephanie started to say.

"Of course she is!" Hannah interrupted. "Anyone who knows how to jump loves doing it. Not everybody is a fraidy-cat like you."

Nicole made a face. "I'm scared of horses," she admitted to Stephanie. "When we were little, Hannah tried to get me to take lessons. I broke out in hives!"

Stephanie laughed. "How can you be afraid of them? Horses are so sweet and beautiful!"

Nicole rolled her eyes. "Oh, no," she teased. "You sound just like Hannah."

"Finally! Someone who likes horses as much as I do." Hannah cried. She shot Stephanie a mournful look. "Obviously, the rest of my friends totally don't get it," she added.

"I know just what you mean," Stephanie said. "My friends aren't scared of horses, but they're not crazy about them, either. It's nice to talk to someone like you about riding."

"I have a bunch of riding magazines I can show you," Hannah offered. "And if you need to borrow any of my equipment, just let me know."

"Thanks." Stephanie noticed Hailey and Jenna— two more of Hannah's friends—approaching the table.

Uh-oh, Stephanie thought. She still hadn't told Hannah which riding class she was in—and now there were *three* other girls listening!

Hailey and Jenna plopped down at the table. "Oh, no—are you talking about horses *again*, Hannah?" Jenna teased.

Hannah grinned. "Yup! Now that Stephanie is riding at my stable, I won't have to bore you guys with stories about Ripley all the time," she answered.

Hannah turned to Stephanie and smiled. "Now

Steph and I can *both* bore you to death talking about horses! Right, Steph?"

"Right," Stephanie smiled back.

I think I'll get Darcy, Allie, and Anna to eat lunch with Hannah and her friends tomorrow, she thought. *This is so much fun. And Hannah and I have so much in common!*

"Nice trotting!" Cora told Stephanie the next afternoon. She pulled her horse, Stargazer, to a walk beside Thunderbolt.

Stephanie pressed her legs against Thunderbolt's sides and gave the reins a few quick pulls to slow him to a walk. "Thanks," she replied. "Thunderbolt's really easy to ride. He does exactly what I want him to."

"That's because he trusts you," Cora said.

Thunderbolt whinnied. He seemed to be agreeing with Cora.

Cora and Stephanie laughed as the rest of the class caught up with them.

"So what's next for today?" Stephanie asked.

"I think it's time to head in," Cora replied.

"Already?" Stephanie groaned in disappointment. Her second lesson had been better than the first one. But they hadn't done anything more than ride around the ring.

"Well, we have only ten minutes to brush the horses and clean the tack," Cora said.

Stephanie was surprised to realize it was so late. She glanced toward the fence. Allie was waiting for her. Stephanie waved, then reluctantly dismounted. She turned Thunderbolt toward the stable.

Allie fell into step with Stephanie as she led Thunderbolt toward his box. "How was class?" she asked.

"Not bad." Stephanie reached up to pat Thunderbolt's neck. "I still wish I were in a jumping class. But dressage is totally amazing. It's all about learning how to communicate with your horse. It's like doing ballet on horseback."

Stephanie gently unlatched Thunderbolt's cinch and pulled off his saddle. "Right, boy?" she asked. "We're learning how to understand each other!"

Thunderbolt thrust his nose into Stephanie's hand. She laughed. "You're looking for carrots, aren't you?" She pulled a carrot out of her sweatshirt pocket and fed it to the horse. While he ate, she removed his saddle blanket and bridle.

Allie leaned against the box door to watch Stephanie work. "Did you decide what to get Becky for her birthday yet?"

"No." Stephanie took a brush off a hook on the wall and began to brush the dirt and sweat from Thunderbolt's black coat. "I asked my dad for ideas last night—and he suggested a mop!"

"No way!" Allie giggled. "He has the same

problem as Michelle. He's thinking of what *he* wants."

"That's exactly what I told him!" Stephanie made sure Thunderbolt didn't have any knots in his tail. At the dude ranch, Stephanie had learned that it was important to groom the horses well. Otherwise, they could end up with skin infections.

Cora came by to check Stephanie's work. "Looks good," she said. "You can go now. See you next time."

"Thanks, Cora!" Stephanie leaned forward and gave Thunderbolt a quick kiss on the nose. "See you on Tuesday," she told the horse. "Let's go!" she added to Allie.

The girls headed outside. Stephanie glanced toward the road. Danny hadn't arrived yet.

"Let's go to the riding ring and watch Hannah's lesson until Dad gets here," Stephanie suggested. "This is her last afternoon lesson. She told me that she's made up all the others she missed because of the flu."

"Cool," Allie agreed. She climbed up on the fence and sat down to watch Hannah in the ring. "Hannah and Ripley are amazing," she said.

Stephanie nodded. Hannah seemed perfectly in control even when Ripley lunged over an enormous jump. "I wish I could jump like that," Stephanie said.

"You can."

Stephanie whirled around. Clint, the junior instructor, stood near the stable door. He wore yellow rubber boots and held a pitchfork. *Mucking gear*, Stephanie thought. *Yuck. I'm glad that students here don't have to help clean out boxes.*

"What did you say?" Stephanie asked.

"I said you *can* jump like that," Clint told her.

Allie shot Stephanie a puzzled look.

"How?" Stephanie asked.

"I'll teach you," Clint offered. "I'm an all-state jumping champion. And I just got my instructor's seal."

"Really? Great!" Stephanie grinned at Allie. "This is like a dream come true. I'm going to learn to jump!"

"That *is* great. . . ." Allie lowered her voice. "But, um, where are you going to get the money for private lessons?"

"Money?" Oops! Stephanie thought. *I knew it sounded too good to be true.*

She turned to Clint. "Actually, my friend is right. I didn't realize you were talking about private lessons. I definitely can't afford that."

Clint frowned. He kicked a rock with his chunky boot. "Oh. Well, sorry."

"Me, too." Stephanie watched miserably as Clint turned away. He slung the pitchfork over his shoulder and walked slowly back toward the stables. He muttered to himself as he went.

"Why is he talking to himself?" Allie whispered.

Stephanie shrugged. "One of his jobs is to muck out all the boxes—you know, clean out the used straw and stuff. He really hates it." She had seen him raking out the boxes a few times. He always looked grumpy as he did it.

"That's it!" Stephanie cried.

"What's it?" Allie asked in confusion.

"Mucking!" Stephanie answered as she hurried after Clint. "Wait!" she called. "Maybe we can make a deal."

Clint looked surprised. "What kind of deal?"

"If you give me private jumping lessons, I'll help you muck out the boxes," Stephanie offered.

"I hate mucking out!" Clint exclaimed.

"Well, now you won't have to do it anymore!" Stephanie told him. "Or at least not as much. How about this—I'll clean out all the boxes each time you give me a lesson?"

"You're on!" Clint said.

"Steph?" Allie looked at Stephanie as if she had lost her mind. "Doesn't mucking out mean cleaning up horse poop? I mean, er . . ."

"Manure!" Stephanie giggled. "I know, it's totally gross. But if it means I can learn to jump . . ." She turned to Clint. "When can we start?"

Clint shrugged. "How's tomorrow afternoon?"

"Tomorrow is terrific!" Stephanie exclaimed. "I

don't have a class with Cora, so I can meet you right after school."

"Great—it's a deal."

Clint smiled and disappeared into the stables. Stephanie spun around in a little circle. "This is perfect!" she cried. "I'm going to learn how to jump—just like Hannah!"

"That's so cool, Steph," Allie told her.

Stephanie nodded. "And you know what else I just thought of? Now I don't have to tell Hannah I'm in the beginners' class."

"What?" Allie cried in surprise. "I thought you told her that yesterday at lunch."

Stephanie frowned. "Well, I was going to. I mean, I tried. But then all her friends were there, and we started talking about horses. . . . And I guess I just forgot. But it's not as if I lied to her."

"No, I guess not," Allie agreed. "But if she misunderstood you, and you didn't set her straight, isn't it *almost* like lying?"

"Well, not anymore!" Stephanie declared. "Because now I'm telling her the truth. I really am taking jumping lessons!"

CHAPTER
5

◆ ◀ ◆ ◆

"Saddle him up," Clint told Stephanie on Wednesday afternoon.

Stephanie nodded. She could hardly wait for her first private lesson to start.

She eased Thunderbolt's saddle on over his blanket and pulled the cinch tight—but not too tight. Then she slipped the bridle over Thunderbolt's nose and put the bit in his mouth.

"Finished?" Clint asked.

Stephanie glanced over her work and then nodded confidently.

"Looks good," Clint said. "But for jumping, the stirrups need to be higher." He quickly moved them up several inches.

As Clint fixed the stirrups, he continued to tell Stephanie the basics about jumping. "You're going to have to get used to some new moves," he said. "But don't worry. You'll master them quickly. Now, do you know how to trot?"

"Of course," Stephanie said.

"Can you post?" Clint asked.

"Yup," she answered. A posting trot was when you held yourself up off the saddle with your legs. Cora had made the beginners' class practice posting for about fifteen minutes the day before. Stephanie's thighs were still sore.

"Good," Clint said. "Climb on."

Stephanie wiped her hands on her jeans. She took Thunderbolt's reins from Clint and mounted. The higher stirrups forced her to bend her knees more than usual, which felt uncomfortable. She squirmed around a little, trying to adjust to the new position. An image of Hannah leaping over five-foot-high jumps popped into her mind.

I'm about to jump! Stephanie thought.

Suddenly she felt a little scared. She wasn't sure she could keep her seat if Thunderbolt jumped a high fence. Especially not with the stirrups raising her legs up in this awkward position.

Clint doesn't have much experience teaching, Stephanie thought. *I hope he realizes I'm a beginner.*

"Um . . . how high did you set the jumps?" Stephanie asked.

"Jumps?" Clint burst out laughing. "We're not jumping today! We'll start with poles on the ground. You have to get used to stepping over them."

"Oh." Stephanie felt a mix of disappointment and relief. She wanted to jump for real. But maybe it would be a good idea to get used to this new way of sitting first.

Clint spaced six red and white poles on the ground, with about five feet between each pole. "Okay!" he called to Stephanie. "Start by walking him over the poles."

Stephanie squeezed Thunderbolt with her knees to signal a walk. The horse immediately moved forward, tossing his head. When they reached the first of the poles, Thunderbolt daintily stepped over it.

This is easy! Stephanie thought.

When Stephanie had walked Thunderbolt over all the poles, Clint motioned for her to join him by the fence.

"Good job," he told her. "Now do it again—but this time think about your center of gravity. You need to have a very solid seat while jumping."

Stephanie walked Thunderbolt over the poles several more times. Then Clint spread the poles farther apart. Stephanie trotted Thunderbolt over them.

Thunderbolt nimbly lifted his legs, easily clearing the poles. Stephanie couldn't help but feel proud of the beautiful horse. *He knows exactly what to do,* Stephanie thought. *Even without any help from me!*

"How did that feel?" Clint called after Stephanie and Thunderbolt had trotted through the course several times.

"Good!"

Clint's wide mouth spread into a smile. "It *looked* good, too. You were lifting yourself out of the saddle as Thunderbolt stepped over the poles. I didn't tell you to do that."

"Sorry!" Stephanie exclaimed. "I didn't even realize I was lifting up. I can—"

Clint waved his hand at her. "Don't worry!" he interrupted with a laugh. "Lifting up is exactly the right thing to do. You're a natural jumper, Stephanie."

Stephanie sat up straighter in the saddle. "Thanks," she said. "So what should we do next?"

"Next we should muck out stalls," Clint said.

Stephanie blinked in surprise. "Already? But we just started."

Clint chuckled. "We started over an hour ago," he told her. "Didn't you say you had to be home by six?"

"On the dot," Stephanie admitted. "My dad is really strict about dinnertime. But it's only four-thirty now."

"Well, you've got at least an hour's worth of

work ahead of you," Clint said. "And that leaves you only half an hour to get home."

"I guess we'd better head in," Stephanie agreed. She dismounted and led Thunderbolt into the stable. She couldn't believe her first jumping lesson was already over. *I didn't realize I would have to spend so much time mucking out*, she thought.

After she had brushed Thunderbolt down, Clint showed her the tack room, where all the horses' gear was kept.

The tiny room was tucked away at one end of the stable. Stephanie couldn't believe how much was crammed into the small space: saddles, saddle blankets, saddle soap, buckets, pitchforks, brooms, sponges, combs, and hoof picks.

"A lot of the horses are out now," Clint told Stephanie. "So it's a perfect time to clean out their boxes."

"What should I do first?" Stephanie asked.

"For today, just use the pitchfork to pick up the manure," Clint instructed her. "It's used as fertilizer in the rest of the park. We pile it up behind the stable."

"Should I put down new straw?" Stephanie asked.

Clint shook his head. "We always replace the straw and wash down the box walls on Friday. But I can tell you more about that in a few days. That is, if you want to come back for another private lesson."

"Definitely!" Stephanie cried.

Clint smiled. "Great. How about Friday afternoon?"

"Perfect." Stephanie picked up a pitchfork. "Well, I'd better get to work." She marched to the closest empty box, dreading the smelly job ahead of her. She opened the door and stared at the clumps of manure littering the hay.

How totally disgusting! Stephanie thought. But she squared her shoulders, scooped up the manure with her pitchfork, and headed outside with it.

It doesn't matter how stinky or gross this is, she told herself. *It will all be worth it when I learn how to jump. Maybe Hannah and I can be in a class together next term.*

For her first few trips Stephanie made sure to breathe through her mouth. But after she had been back and forth a couple of times, she took a sniff. It wasn't that bad. Nowhere near as bad as dirty diapers.

In fact, Stephanie liked the stable smells: the odors of horses, hay, and leather all mixed together. She fell into the rhythm of her work, almost feeling like a member of the stable staff.

This whole deal is working out great, Stephanie thought with satisfaction. *Clint's a good teacher.*

Mucking out isn't so awful. And I bet I'll be jumping as well as Hannah in no time.

During Thursday afternoon's class Stephanie watched carefully as Lily rode her horse in a figure eight. *Sloppy left-hand turn*, Stephanie noted. *Thunderbolt and I have this move down perfectly.*

Thunderbolt snorted and tossed his head as if he could read Stephanie's thoughts.

"I know, boy," Stephanie murmured. "You're impatient, too. You and I both want to do something more challenging."

"Not bad," Cora told Lily. "But remember to keep the reins tight. Watch how Stephanie does it."

Cora nodded at Stephanie.

Stephanie gave Thunderbolt a gentle squeeze with her legs. Thunderbolt moved smoothly through the figure eight.

"Perfect!" Cora called.

"Thanks," Stephanie said. "Can we move on to the next figure?"

"Maybe on Saturday," Cora answered. "But now I want everybody to cool down the horses. We'll regroup in the stable. Good class, kids!"

Stephanie dismounted and led Thunderbolt around the ring until the horse's breathing slowed. "It's a good thing you and I are taking private lessons with Clint," she told Thunderbolt. "Otherwise this baby class would be unbearable!"

She put Thunderbolt back into his box and followed Lily and the others to the office, where Cora was waiting for them.

"I have some terrific news for you." Cora's dark eyes shone with excitement. "The Golden Gate Riding Academy is hosting a special Christmas horse show. It will be a week from Saturday!"

"Are we invited?" Lily asked.

Cora grinned at her. "You're not just invited— you're the stars of the show."

"What do you mean?" Janie asked.

"Well, each class at the stable will compete in the show," Cora explained. "So this will be your first competition!"

Stephanie couldn't believe it. A competition? Her class had barely done any riding! "But we've been taking lessons for only a few weeks," she protested.

"You've already learned enough to compete in Level One dressage," Cora said. "You'll have to walk and trot your horses around in circles of different sizes. Plus, you'll do some figures—like the one we were working on today."

"Wow," Lily cried. "That sounds cool."

"It will be," Cora said. "So make sure you invite all of your family and friends to cheer for you."

Stephanie bit her lip. Invite people? She hadn't even thought about anyone coming to *watch* the horse show. It would be totally embarrassing to let her friends see her riding with a bunch of ten-year-olds.

"I'm going to invite my whole class," Christie announced.

I'm not, Stephanie thought. *I'm not even going to tell my friends about this horse show. In fact, I don't think I'll even invite my family!*

"Are there going to be prizes?" Lily asked.

Cora nodded. "We'll give out ribbons for the three top scores in each category."

"Cool," Stephanie said. Maybe this horse show *would* be kind of fun—since nobody she knew would be watching.

"Stephanie will win everything," Janie complained. "She's totally the best person in our class."

The other girls nodded in agreement.

Cora shot Stephanie a smile. "Don't give up so easily," she told Janie. "Maybe Stephanie will have an off day."

"I hope so—I want a ribbon!" Lily announced.

Stephanie couldn't help laughing.

"Even if you don't win a ribbon, the show will still be good experience for you," Cora went on. "And you'll get to see what all the other classes are working on."

Stephanie stopped laughing. Suddenly she realized what Cora had just said. *Other* classes? Her eyes widened in horror.

"Wait!" Stephanie cried. "You mean the other dressage classes, right?"

Cora shook her head. "Everyone who rides here at the academy will be in the show. All the classes are involved."

Stephanie took a shaky breath. "What about private students?" she asked.

"Them, too," Cora replied. "Even some of the instructors participate in the show. That's what makes it so much fun."

"Yeah, fun," Stephanie muttered.

All the riders at the stable would be at the show. Including the girls in the jumping classes. Including private students.

Including Hannah.

I can't let Hannah see me compete with the beginning class, Stephanie thought with horror. *She thinks I'm in Intermediate Jumping! She'll think I lied to her on purpose!*

What am I going to do now?

CHAPTER
6

◆ ◀ ◗ ◆

"Steph! Move it! You'll be late for school!" D.J. called up the stairs on Friday morning.

Stephanie rolled over on her side. She opened one eye to look at the clock: 7:25. She glanced across the room. Michelle's bed was already empty.

"No, no, no . . ." Stephanie groaned out loud. *I can't believe I overslept!* she thought. Now she had exactly ten minutes to dress and eat breakfast before the school bus left.

"Ouch," Stephanie moaned as she climbed out of bed. She rubbed her thigh gingerly. *My leg muscles are so sore*, she thought. *In fact, all my muscles are sore.*

"Riding lessons three days in a row is definitely too much," Stephanie told herself. She hobbled down the hall to the bathroom. She put some toothpaste on her toothbrush and glanced long-ingly at the tub.

There was no time for a long hot bath now, she realized. So she promised one to herself after school. But then she remembered she had a jumping lesson with Clint that afternoon. Stephanie sighed. Maybe she could take a bath after dinner.

After quickly washing her face and combing her hair, Stephanie hurried back to her room. *I hope I have something clean to wear,* she thought. She had been spending so much time at the stables that she was behind on her chores. She'd meant to do laundry the night before. But she'd been too tired when she got home.

Stephanie was pulling on an old pair of jeans when D.J. poked her head into the room.

"Check out the decorations I got for Becky's party," D.J. said.

Stephanie took a quick look at the red and green balloons and streamers D.J. held. Then she pulled open one of her dresser drawers. She felt certain she had a clean T-shirt somewhere. "Those are nice." Stephanie said. "But Becky likes purple."

"I know," D.J. answered. "But Becky thinks we're planning a Christmas party, remember? She'd think it was weird if we had purple decorations for Christmas."

"I guess," Stephanie mumbled.

"I'm giving her a purple scarf for her birthday," D.J. went on. "What did you get?"

"Nothing yet," Stephanie groaned.

The only clean T-shirt she could find was white. *Boring*, Stephanie thought. But then she noticed the clock—7:33. She had exactly two minutes to get dressed, grab some food, and catch the bus. She yanked the T-shirt out and pulled it on.

"What about Michelle?" D.J. asked. "Did you help her find a present for Becky?"

"Not yet." Stephanie looked at her reflection in the mirror. *What a boring outfit*, she thought with disgust. *Maybe I can do something special with my hair on the bus.*

"The party is next week," D.J. pointed out. "You don't have much time to shop."

Stephanie picked up her book bag. "I know," she said, heading out the door. "I'll take Michelle shopping again soon. See you later."

Stephanie galloped down the stairs, grabbed an apple for breakfast, tucked her lunch into her book bag, and ran outside. She got to the bus stop just in time to catch the late bus.

"Stephanie!" Nicole Harwood called down the crowded hallway. She wore slim black trousers and a crushed velvet sweater. Totally hip, Stephanie thought. Unlike *my* outfit today.

"Hi, Nicole," Stephanie said.

"How are your riding lessons?" Nicole asked as she fell into step beside Stephanie.

"Great!" Just thinking about the stable was enough to make Stephanie smile.

"I'm totally excited about the riding show," Nicole went on.

Stephanie turned to stare at Nicole. "You mean the Christmas riding show? You know about that?"

"Sure," Nicole said. "Hailey and I go every Christmastime to cheer for Hannah. And this year we'll have *two* show jumpers to cheer for."

"Um, two?" Stephanie mumbled. She felt a little sick.

"Sure—Hannah and you," Nicole said. "Oh, hey—here's my class. See you!"

"Yeah. Bye," Stephanie answered. She kept walking down the hall, but she could barely remember what classroom she was heading for.

"Listen," Nicole called after her. "Tell Darcy and Allie they can come with us to the show if they want to."

"Oh, right. Thanks," Stephanie called back. *This is terrible,* she thought. *This is a nightmare.* It was bad enough that Hannah would see her competing with the baby class. But now all Hannah's friends would see it, too!

Stephanie glanced at her watch. *I've got to see Darcy and Allie right away,* she thought. *They've got to help me find a way out of this mess.*

51

She began running down the hall toward the pay phones, where she met her friends every morning. But she had gone only a few yards when Wendy Gorell jumped in front of her. Wendy was kind of nerdy. And she was the exact opposite of Nicole— she had terrible taste in clothes. Today Wendy wore purple corduroys and an orange turtleneck.

"Stephanie! I just heard." Wendy exclaimed. "I'm so excited for you."

"Sorry, Wendy," Stephanie said, trying to move around the other girl. "I'm kind of in a hurry."

"Oh, no biggie," Wendy said. "I'm in a hurry, too. I'm going to read the homeroom announcements over the P.A. today. The members of the audiovisual club are taking turns. And today's my turn."

"That's nice." Stephanie started down the hall again. But suddenly she realized what Wendy had just said. She quickly spun around. "Wait!" she cried. "*What* did you just hear?"

"About the Christmas horse show," Wendy exclaimed. "Hailey told me you're definitely going to win a ribbon. That's so exciting that I decided to tell everyone about it during announcements."

Panicked, Stephanie grabbed Wendy's arm. "No! You can't say anything about the horse show."

"Why not?" Wendy asked.

"Because . . . because it will make me nervous to

have a bunch of kids from school there," Stephanie blurted out.

Wendy shrugged. "Okay, Stephanie, if you don't want me to read the flyer, I won't."

"Flyer?" Stephanie repeated.

"Yeah," Wendy said. She held out a bright yellow paper.

Stephanie grabbed the flyer and stared at it in horror. GOLDEN GATE RIDING ACADEMY'S ANNUAL CHRISTMAS HORSE SHOW. GENERAL PUBLIC WELCOME. At the bottom someone had written: *Starring John Muir's Jumpers, Stephanie Tanner and Hannah Marsh! Come See Your Classmates Bring Home Blue Ribbons.*

Stephanie took a deep breath. It would have been a disaster if Wendy read this flyer out loud to the entire school.

"Thanks for not announcing this," Stephanie said. "I really get terrible stage fright."

"That's okay," Wendy said. "But I think people are going to come to your show anyway."

"Why?"

Wendy pointed down the hallway. Stephanie's heart sank. Yellow flyers were taped to every classroom door. "Hannah Marsh is putting those up all over school," Wendy explained.

I'm doomed, Stephanie thought. *Totally doomed.*

Now the entire school would see her riding with a bunch of little kids. Even worse, Hannah might tell everyone that she lied about being in the jumping class.

What am I going to do?

"Listen, Wendy, I'll see you later," Stephanie said.

"Bye," Wendy called as Stephanie jogged down the almost-deserted hallway.

Stephanie felt as if she might cry with relief when she saw Allie and Darcy still standing in their usual spot near the pay phones.

"Did you guys see this?" Stephanie waved the flyer above her head as she hurried up to her friends.

"Only about a million times," Darcy said. "Hannah is hanging them everywhere. There are at least six in the bathroom."

Stephanie slumped against the wall. "What am I going to do?" she moaned. "Hannah invited all her friends to the show. And they expect me to compete with the intermediate jumping class. I've got to do something. And you guys have to help me."

"This is awful." Allie's green eyes were sympathetic. "I wish Hannah had never misunderstood you!"

"Me, too," Stephanie cried. "But what am I going to do now?"

Allie chewed on her lip thoughtfully. "You could still tell Hannah the truth," she pointed out.

Stephanie tried to imagine Hannah's reaction to the truth—and she couldn't imagine anything very good. She shook her head. "It's too late for that. I've already been pretending to know how to jump."

"You could pretend to be sick the day of the horse show," Darcy suggested.

Stephanie shook her head again. "Fooling my dad is impossible. Unless you can think of a way to actually make me sick, we have to think of something else."

"Like what?" Allie asked. "Everyone expects you to jump with the intermediate class. And you know that's impossible."

Stephanie began to pace up and down in front of her friends. "Maybe it's not *completely* impossible," she said.

Darcy raised one eyebrow. "Uh-oh. I've seen that look before. What are you planning, Steph?"

"Maybe if I doubled up on my classes with Clint . . ." Stephanie's mind was working overtime. "I could learn to jump really fast. Then I'll demonstrate for Cora. She told me she would consider moving me up early. And when she sees how good I am, she'll have to let me into the intermediate jumping class!"

"Not a bad plan," Darcy said with a grin.

Allie put one hand on her hip. "Not bad—except for one thing. The Christmas riding show is in one week. You can't learn all of that before next Saturday, Steph."

"I can try," Stephanie answered.

"Go for it!" Darcy said.

"I will!"

Stephanie knew her plan was a long shot. *But I'll make it work*, she promised herself. *I have to.*

CHAPTER
7

◆ ◀ ◢ ◆

"Ready for your lesson?" Clint asked that afternoon.

"Absolutely!" Stephanie told him. *Except that my muscles are so sore, I can hardly walk,* she added silently.

But Stephanie knew her sore legs didn't matter. All that mattered was learning how to jump—as fast as possible.

"Go saddle up Thunderbolt and meet me in the ring," Clint said.

"Okay." Stephanie walked into the stable and hurried to Thunderbolt's box.

Thunderbolt whinnied when he saw her.

"Hello, beautiful," Stephanie murmured, running her hand along Thunderbolt's neck. The tall black horse pushed his muzzle against her shoulder.

Suddenly Stephanie felt happier than she had all day. *Thunderbolt will get me out of this mess*, she thought. *He already knows how to jump. All I have to do is let him teach me.*

"Are you ready to have some fun?" Stephanie asked the horse. Thunderbolt tossed his head back and pawed the ground with his hoof.

Stephanie smiled. "Me, too. Let's go get Clint."

She led Thunderbolt out of his box and carefully saddled him up. Stephanie couldn't help groaning as she put her left foot in the stirrup and swung herself up into the saddle. *Don't be a baby*, she told herself. *Sore muscles won't kill you.*

"Come on, boy!" She squeezed Thunderbolt with her knees and they walked out into the ring.

Stephanie spotted Clint near the stables, pulling several long metal bars out of a supply shed. "Take him around the ring a few times to warm him up," he called to Stephanie. "Start with a walk. Then trot him."

"Okay!" Stephanie guided Thunderbolt around the ring. As they circled, she watched Clint. He was setting the metal bars into brackets made of crisscrossed pieces of wood. The bars hung about six inches off the ground.

After Thunderbolt was warmed up, Stephanie

eagerly turned him toward Clint. "What are those bars?" Stephanie asked.

Clint brushed his bangs out of his eyes. "They're called cavalletti. Running Thunderbolt through them is your first step toward jumping."

"Finally," Stephanie said. "I can't wait." She studied the cavalletti. They didn't look exactly like fences—but they were close. Her plan to become a show jumper by next Saturday was right on schedule.

"Okay, let's go," Clint said in a businesslike tone. "You're going to take Thunderbolt over these at a walk. Aim for the lowest point. I've set the cavalletti at about eight inches high—so it should be easy."

They look higher than that, Stephanie thought. But she didn't say anything. She didn't have time to be nervous. If she wanted to learn how to jump in time for the horse show, she had to learn as much as she could as fast as she could!

"Thunderbolt will have to lift his legs pretty high to step over these," Clint went on. "Trust him. He knows what he's doing. Your job is to lift yourself up out of the saddle as Thunderbolt clears the cavalletti. So you have to move with his movement."

Stephanie bit her lower lip and nodded. "Okay."

Thunderbolt lifted his head. His nostrils flared.

Clint laughed and gave him an affectionate pat on the neck. "Thunderbolt's ready. Are you?"

"Sure," Stephanie said with more confidence than she felt. She turned Thunderbolt around and headed him toward the first cavalletti.

Just don't fall off, Stephanie told herself. Her heart pounded as Thunderbolt reached the first set of poles. His broad back rose as he delicately lifted his front hooves over the poles.

Stephanie shut her eyes and clung to the reins. *Don't fall!* she thought again. She waited to feel the bounce when Thunderbolt's back hooves landed.

Nothing happened.

Stephanie opened her eyes and gasped. Thunderbolt was already halfway to the next cavalletti. Stephanie hadn't even noticed the horse's back legs hitting the ground.

That wasn't so bad, she thought. *In fact, it was fun—just a little hop!*

"Don't forget to lift yourself up," Clint called to her from the fence. "Do your job."

Stephanie felt much more in control as Thunderbolt approached the second set of poles. She rose in the stirrups as Thunderbolt stepped over the next cavalletti. He cleared them easily. By the time they reached the third set, Stephanie knew exactly when Thunderbolt was going to jump. She rose in the saddle at the perfect moment.

As they cleared the last cavalletti, Stephanie

broke into a wide smile. She reached down to pat Thunderbolt between the ears.

"You're having as much fun as I am, aren't you?" she asked as they turned back toward Clint.

Thunderbolt snorted as if to say yes.

"How was that?" Stephanie called to Clint. She felt proud of how well she had handled her first run.

Clint made a face. "Not bad, I guess. But you forgot to lift yourself up on the first cavalletti. And on the second one you stood up on the stirrups. That puts a lot of weight on Thunderbolt's back. Next time use your legs to hold yourself up. Push against Thunderbolt's sides."

"No problem," Stephanie said. She didn't feel even a little bit nervous anymore. *Jumping is just as great as Hannah said*, she thought. *I bet Thunderbolt and I will be doing real jumps by my next lesson.*

For the next hour. Stephanie walked Thunderbolt through the cavalletti dozens of times. "Good work," Clint told her at the end of the lesson.

"Thanks." Stephanie fought an urge to slump in the saddle. The cavalletti were only six inches high, but she was exhausted. Her muscles were more sore than ever.

"When can we have another lesson?" she asked as she slowly dismounted.

"How about next Wednesday?" Clint suggested.

"But today's Friday! That's five days away,"

Stephanie protested. *I can't afford to waste that much time!*

"Can't we have one this weekend?" she asked. "How about tomorrow?"

"Don't you have a class with Cora tomorrow?" Clint asked.

"Yeah," Stephanie answered. "In the morning. But we could have a lesson after my class."

Clint frowned. "Why don't you rest for a few days?" he asked. "After all the time you've been spending in the saddle, your leg muscles must be killing you."

"Only every now and then," Stephanie fibbed. *Like whenever I move,* she added silently.

Clint shrugged. "Fine with me. A lesson for you means less mucking out for me. You can come every day if you want," he joked.

"I would if I could jump every day," Stephanie told him with a smile.

"Okay," Clint said. "But no private lessons this weekend—Cora will yell at me if you're too tired for her class. Why don't you rest on Sunday and come back on Monday?"

"Great," Stephanie said as she led Thunderbolt toward the stable. "Can we try a real jump then?"

Clint held open the stable door for her. "Probably not."

"What?" Stephanie stopped walking. "Why not?"

"Because it's important to master the basics first," Clint replied. "And you still have a little way to go."

"Oh," Stephanie said. She tried not to feel disappointed. *Cora said the same thing about learning the basics,* she thought. *I just hope learning the basics doesn't take more than a week.*

"So, are those boots waterproof?" Clint asked.

Stephanie looked down at her boots. "I think so—why?"

Clint's blue eyes twinkled. "Because today is the day we wash down the boxes and give the horses new straw. Friday—remember?"

Stephanie groaned. She'd forgotten she still had all that hard work to do. *I wonder what would happen if I collapsed right here in the straw?* she thought.

"Brush Thunderbolt down and sweep out the empty boxes," Clint told her. "Then I'll show you where to find the hose and clean straw."

"No problem," Stephanie said with as much energy as she could muster.

I am not tired, she told herself as she started to unbuckle Thunderbolt's saddle. *If I'm going to learn how to jump by next Saturday, I don't have time to be tired.*

CHAPTER
8

◆ ◀ ▪ ◆

"Did you have fun at class?" Becky asked. Stephanie had just gotten home on Saturday afternoon.

"Uh-huh," Stephanie mumbled. "I love riding."

But right now I'm too tired to even talk about horses, she added silently.

Cora had spent that day's class getting the girls ready for the horse show. They had learned how to walk their horses into the ring, stop, and salute the judges. The exercise had been fun.

But the only thing Stephanie could concentrate on was what Hannah and all her friends would think when they saw her ride into the show with the baby class.

They'll think I'm a liar, she realized. *They'll all think I purposely lied about being in the jumping class.*

And then they'll laugh at me for being with a bunch of little kids.

"Where should I put these cookie sheets?" Becky's voice broke into Stephanie's thoughts. She glanced up to see her aunt standing on a footstool, helping Danny put away groceries. Stephanie looked around in surprise. The kitchen table was covered with bags of food. So were all the counters.

Oops, Stephanie thought. Her dad and Becky had obviously been shopping all day, and she was just sitting there without even helping them.

"Let me put the food away," Stephanie offered. *The laundry can wait for another half an hour*, she decided. *And so can my homework.*

"Thanks," Danny said. "The stuff on the end of the table belongs in the fridge."

Stephanie picked up a gallon of milk and headed toward the refrigerator. Just as she reached for the handle, a familiar yellow flyer caught her eye. It was stuck to the fridge with a horse-shaped magnet. GOLDEN GATE RIDING ACADEMY'S ANNUAL CHRISTMAS HORSE SHOW, Stephanie read.

Her heart sank. It was bad enough that the flyer was up all over school. Now her whole family would see it, too.

"Where did you get this?" she asked her father.

"Oh, it came in the mail this morning," Danny

answered. "Why didn't you tell us about the show, sweetie?"

Because I don't want anyone to know about it, Stephanie thought miserably. "I guess I just forgot," she said. "And it's really no big deal. You don't have to go."

Danny put an arm around Stephanie's shoulder. "Of course we're going!"

"I can't wait," Becky put in. "I want to see my early Christmas present in action."

"There's not going to be much for you to see," Stephanie said. "I am only a beginner, you know."

"Well, everybody has to start somewhere," Becky said. "We don't expect you to be an expert rider."

"Right," Danny said. "We just want you to have fun."

"Have fun doing what?" Michelle asked as she walked into the kitchen.

"Going to my horse show," Stephanie murmured. She was beginning to feel sick. "The whole family is going."

"I'm sick of your horse lessons," Michelle complained. "You're always at the stables. You haven't cleaned your half of the room in a week!"

Stephanie cringed. Her room really must be a mess if Michelle was complaining about it.

"I know. I'll do it soon," she promised.

"You *are* spending a lot of time at the riding

academy, honey," Danny said. "I thought your lessons were only three days a week."

Oh, no, Stephanie thought. *How am I going to explain all this to Dad? He doesn't even know about my private jumping lessons.*

"Um, I'm doing some extra practice," she said. "You know—for the horse show."

"I remember how hard I used to work before competitions," Becky agreed. "I practically lived at the stables."

"Well, I'm sure your practice will all be worth it, Steph," Danny said. "Your horse show is going to be fun for all of us."

"The whole day will be great," Becky declared. "Your show is the morning of our Christmas party. So we get to watch you ride in the morning, and then we can bring all your friends home with us from the riding show. That way, they won't need rides to the party!"

Stephanie tried not to laugh. Becky was so excited about the Christmas party—imagine how she would feel when she realized it was a birthday party for *her*!

"Jesse may have to leave a little early to let people in," Danny said. He winked at Stephanie behind Becky's back. "But he promises to stay long enough to see you compete. And Joey is going to take pictures."

"Oh. Great," Stephanie said.

This is a nightmare, she thought. Things just kept getting worse and worse. Everyone in the whole world was going to see her make a fool of herself.

Plus, if her family came to the show, she would have to explain why she was riding with the intermediate jumping class instead of the beginners. *I hope Becky isn't insulted that I moved out of the class she signed me up for*, Stephanie thought. It had never occurred to her that her family would find out which riding class she was taking.

"I'm going to put some Christmas music on," Becky announced. She pushed through the kitchen door and headed into the living room.

"Speaking of the party," Danny said when she was gone, "we only have one week to pull everything together. Let's check our to-do list." He went to the counter, where his briefcase was tucked up against the wall. He pulled out a legal pad and a pen.

"Decorations?" Danny read.

"D.J. got them," Stephanie told him. "Becky thinks they're Christmas decorations."

"Check!" Danny made a mark on the pad. "Presents? I've got mine. How about you guys?"

Michelle frowned at Stephanie.

"Not yet," Stephanie admitted. "I've been too busy at the stables. But we'll definitely get something great before next weekend."

Michelle rolled her eyes. But she didn't say anything.

"Okay," Danny agreed. "Just don't leave it until the last minute. Let's see. . . . The next thing on the list is cake. I'll make that on Friday evening. Jesse and Becky are planning to go out that night." He looked up. "What do you guys think—should I make a chocolate or yellow cake?"

"Chocolate," Stephanie said.

"Yellow," Michelle said at the same time.

Danny laughed. "Well, maybe I'll make both. After all, we are going to have a lot of guests." He flipped through several neatly printed pages of names.

"Cassie and Mandy can both come," Michelle announced. The two girls were her best friends.

"Great!" Danny added them to his list. "That makes forty-seven people who are definitely coming."

"Wow," Michelle said. "Becky's really going to have a terrific birthday."

"What about your guests, Steph?" Danny asked. "Are Allie and Darcy coming?"

"I haven't asked them yet," Stephanie replied.

"Well, don't forget," Danny said. "And you should invite some of your friends from the stable—like that girl Hannah you told us about. She can come straight from the riding show."

"Sure," Stephanie said. *If Hannah is still speaking to me after she finds out I lied*, she added to herself.

"Yum," Stephanie said with a happy sigh. The gooey slice of pizza sitting in front of her was making her mouth water.

She, Darcy, and Allie had decided to meet at Tony's Pizzeria for lunch on Sunday afternoon.

Darcy took a careful bite of her cheesy slice. "So have you learned how to jump yet?" she asked with her mouth full.

"Not yet," Stephanie admitted. "But the good news is that I still have a week left."

"What's the bad news?" Allie asked.

Stephanie hid her face with her hand. "My entire family is coming to the riding show," she said with a groan. "And they're going to be mad at me no matter what."

"How come?" Allie asked.

"Well, let's say I don't get into the jumping class," Stephanie said. "Hannah will see me with the baby class, and she'll be mad at me for lying to her. Then Dad will ask why Hannah isn't coming to our Christmas party—and I'll have to tell him why she's mad."

Darcy nodded. "And he'll yell at you for lying to Hannah," she finished.

"Right," Stephanie said. "But let's say I *do* get into the jumping class. My family will be shocked, because they expect me to be in beginning dressage. And they'll be mad that I switched without telling them."

Allie giggled. "You're getting me confused, Steph! Don't worry so much about your family. They'll be happy to see you jump, if that's what you love to do."

"Especially Becky," Darcy put in. "She was a show jumper, too. She'll understand exactly why you switched classes."

"*If* I switch classes," Stephanie muttered.

"You will," Darcy said. "You're going to learn how to jump and get Cora to move you to the intermediate jumping class."

Stephanie groaned. "Yeah—if I survive that long. My leg muscles are sore from riding. My arm muscles are sore from mucking out the stalls all the time."

Darcy made a face. "I can't believe you have to do that."

Stephanie nodded. "Plus, I'm always tired. The only time I have to do my homework is at night. So I'm not getting any sleep."

"Poor Steph!" Allie cried.

"*And* I have to take Michelle shopping for Becky's birthday present," Stephanie went on. "Which reminds me—you guys are invited. She thinks it's a Christmas party, so she expects us all to invite our friends. It's right after the horse show."

"I'll be there," Darcy said.

"Me, too." Allie took a sip of her soda. "What are you getting her?"

Stephanie rolled her eyes. "I still don't know—I haven't had time to think of anything. Do you have any ideas?"

"Something for work?" Allie suggested.

"She needs a new briefcase," Stephanie said. "But that's way too expensive. Jesse is buying her clothes. And D.J. already got her a scarf."

"How about something for her desk?" Darcy suggested. "Like—um, maybe a nice pen?"

"Boring," Stephanie said, taking another big bite of pizza.

"What about a funny phone?" Allie said. "You could get a race car—or Mickey Mouse."

Stephanie made a face. "I think she's too old for that."

"I know—get her one of those nice boxes to keep photos and stuff in," Darcy suggested. "Becky obviously likes to keep old pictures. Remember that ratty shoe box full of her riding photos and ribbons?"

"That's it!" Stephanie cried. "Darce, you're a genius!"

"Thanks! Becky will love a photo box!" Darcy said.

"No, I'm getting her something even better," Stephanie said with excitement. "Remember when we found that shoe box? Becky said she wanted to make a scrapbook."

"That's right," Allie cried. "So you can get her a really pretty photo album to use as a scrapbook."

"Great idea," Darcy agreed. "I really am a genius!"

Allie rolled her eyes and laughed. Stephanie playfully tossed her napkin at Darcy.

"Well, that's one problem solved," she said. "Now all I have to do is learn how to jump, and Saturday will be a terrific day."

CHAPTER
9

◆ ◀ ◢ ◆

"Are you getting excited about the riding show?" Hannah asked Stephanie on Monday afternoon.

Stephanie sat with Hannah, Nicole, Hailey, Darcy, Anna, and Allie at a table near the cafeteria window. She and her friends had been eating lunch with Hannah every day for the past week.

"*I'm* excited about the show," Anna put in. "Whether Stephanie is or not!"

Stephanie wondered if she should just tell Hannah the truth about her beginners' class. Just the words *riding show* were enough to make a lump form in her throat. But somehow she just couldn't get the words out.

"I guess I'm excited," she told Hannah.

"Well, don't sound too happy," Hannah teased her. "Are you nervous?"

"Definitely. It's all I can think about," Stephanie said. She saw Allie and Darcy exchange a smile.

"Yeah, and it's all she can *talk* about," Darcy teased her.

"Well, listen to this," Hannah said. "I talked *The Scribe* into doing a story on us for the Christmas edition. I promised Sari—she's this girl I know who works for the paper—that she could interview both of us after the horse show."

"That's amazing!" Stephanie exclaimed. "I definitely want to be in *The Scribe.*"

Stephanie imagined her photograph on the front page of the school newspaper. Maybe the paper would even take a picture of her and Hannah together. *That would be totally cool,* Stephanie thought. She had written lots of articles for the paper—but she'd never had a story written *about* her.

"Great! I'm going to get every extra issue of the paper," Hailey reported. "You guys should save a copy of the article as a keepsake."

Just like Becky, Stephanie thought. She reached over and gave Hannah a happy hug. "This is so cool!" she exclaimed. "And thanks so much for including me. You're really a good friend."

"No problem," Hannah said with a grin.

Stephanie felt terrific—until she saw Allie's worried expression. Even Darcy looked a little uncomfortable. She knew what they were thinking: What if she didn't get into the jumping class? What kind of article would *The Scribe* run then?

Well, there's no reason to worry, Stephanie told herself. *So what if everyone comes to the show and the paper does a story on it.*

By that time I'll be in the intermediate jumping class. No matter what.

"Last one, boy," Stephanie whispered to Thunderbolt. She aimed the horse at the final set of cavalletti. He trotted easily over them.

That was a perfect practice run, Stephanie thought. Now Clint would have to let her jump.

She turned Thunderbolt toward the fence, where Clint sat watching. "How was that?" she called.

"Not bad," Clint told her. "But you need to think about keeping your weight centered over Thunderbolt's neck. You're leaning back too far."

"Oh, no!" Stephanie said. "Do I have to run the cavalletti again?"

Clint nodded. "Try it again at a trot. And this time think about staying centered."

We've been practicing cavalletti forever, Stephanie thought as she walked Thunderbolt toward the beginning of the course. *At this rate I'm never going to learn to jump!*

Stephanie gave Thunderbolt a little rein and squeezed her legs against his sides to urge him forward. He trotted toward the poles and hopped over them without breaking stride. As they cleared the jump, Stephanie tried to shift her weight forward.

But before she could get herself centered over his neck, Thunderbolt was already taking the second set of cavalletti. Stephanie was thrown to the left as Thunderbolt lifted his front legs over the pole.

Uh-oh, Stephanie thought. *What do I do now? Lean forward again, or sit up straight until I catch my balance?*

She leaned forward as Thunderbolt trotted toward the last set of poles. While he hopped over, Stephanie clung to the reins, trying to get centered over his neck.

"That's okay," Clint called. "You'll get it. Let's just try the whole thing again at a walk."

Sure, why not? Stephanie thought as she turned Thunderbolt back toward the beginning. *I've got all the time I need—as long as I don't care about the entire world finding out I don't know how to jump!*

The next practice run went a little smoother. But Stephanie was still fighting to find a comfortable position.

"Much better!" Clint called. "But you're starting to lean on the stirrups. Support your own weight. Do it again at a walk."

I'm going to scream! Stephanie thought. But she took a deep breath instead. *Calm down,* she told herself. *Clint's not going to let me jump until I can run these cavalletti perfectly. And that means I have to concentrate.*

As Stephanie walked Thunderbolt to the front of the jumps, she imagined herself taking them perfectly. "Let's do this right," she whispered to the horse.

Thunderbolt took the first jump. Stephanie leaned forward, holding the reins close to his powerful neck. She used her legs to hold herself out of the saddle—and her sore muscles ached. *That must mean I'm doing it the right way*, Stephanie thought. *If I weren't supporting my own weight, my legs wouldn't hurt so much!*

"Nice," Clint called when Stephanie finished the last of the cavalletti. "Let's see that again."

"Did I make any mistakes?" Stephanie called back.

"Nope, it looked good," Clint said.

"Great!" Stephanie cried. "Then let's move on to real jumps!"

"Not yet. I want you to memorize how it's supposed to feel," Clint replied. "It's got to feel so natural that you don't even think of doing it any other way."

Stephanie groaned. "Okay. But can I at least take it at a trot this time?"

Clint shook his head. "Better keep it at a walk for now."

Stephanie turned Thunderbolt back to the front of the cavalletti. She concentrated on remembering the last run, so that she would do it exactly the same way again.

"We have to get this right, Thunderbolt," she told the horse. "Or Clint will never let us take real jumps. And I'll be humiliated in front of my entire school."

Thunderbolt seemed to understand. Stephanie urged him forward. Again she concentrated on holding herself up with her leg muscles and keeping centered over Thunderbolt's neck. The entire run felt perfect.

"Yes!" Stephanie cried. "That was incredible, Thunderbolt!"

"Nice," Clint called. "One more time."

"What?" Stephanie turned Thunderbolt around and trotted him over to Clint. "But I know how to do it," she argued. "I just did it perfectly twice. Won't you please teach me how to jump now?"

"I *am* teaching you to jump," Clint replied. "Running the cavalletti is the first step. It will teach you all the basics of jumping."

"But I want to take real jumps," Stephanie said.

Clint shook his head. "You're not ready for that yet, Stephanie. Why are you in such a hurry?"

Stephanie felt her cheeks get hot. She couldn't tell Clint about her plan, or about the school paper doing an article on her jumping skills. "I just want to jump," she mumbled.

"Well, arguing with me isn't getting you any closer to that goal," Clint said. "But walking through the cavalletti will."

Stephanie sighed in frustration. But she turned Thunderbolt around and headed him back to the jumps. When she got to the beginning, she glanced over at Clint for the signal to start.

But Clint wasn't paying any attention to her. He stood near the door of the stables, talking to one of the other instructors. Suddenly he turned to Stephanie. "Steph, come here," he called.

Stephanie walked Thunderbolt over to see what was going on. "What's up?" she asked.

"I have to go to a meeting with the stable owner," Clint explained. "I'm sorry, Stephanie, but all the instructors are supposed to attend."

"What should I do?" Stephanie asked.

"We have only about five minutes left," Clint said. "Do you mind if we quit early today?"

I don't want to quit until I get to jump, Stephanie thought. "Can't I just run through the cavalletti by myself for the rest of our time?" Stephanie asked.

"No," Clint said. "You can't ride unless I'm watching you. Those are the stable rules."

"All right," Stephanie grumbled. She slowly dismounted and began walking Thunderbolt around the ring to cool him down.

"What should I do, boy?" she asked the horse. "If I'm going to jump on Saturday, I've got to start soon."

Thunderbolt butted his head against Stephanie's shoulder as if to say he understood.

"I have only four days left," Stephanie went on. "And Clint didn't even say when our next lesson would be." She stopped walking and looked up into Thunderbolt's soft brown eyes.

"*You* know how to jump, boy," she murmured. "So why won't Clint let us jump together?"

"Hey, Stephanie!"

Stephanie glanced up—and saw Allie and Darcy standing on the other side of the ring. They were grinning and waving at her.

"Come on, Thunderbolt," Stephanie said. "My friends are here." She led him over to the fence.

"You seemed to be having a real heart-to-heart with your horse," Darcy teased her. "Do you two have a lot to talk about?"

"Thunderbolt is my best friend at the stable," Stephanie replied with a grin. "He's the only one who knows my plan for jumping in the horse show."

"He's really beautiful." Darcy ran her hand over Thunderbolt's neck.

"What are you guys doing here?" Stephanie asked.

"We were blading in the park. And I wanted to

see you in action," Darcy explained. "So we decided to come watch your lesson."

Stephanie frowned. "Well, my lesson is over, unfortunately."

"What's the matter?" Allie asked.

"Clint won't let me jump," Stephanie complained. "He keeps making me hop those cavalletti things over and over."

"Why?" Darcy asked.

"He says I'm not ready to jump yet," Stephanie said. "He says I have to memorize how it feels to jump the cavalletti."

Allie shrugged. "He's the teacher. He must know what he's talking about."

"But I *feel* ready," Stephanie argued. "I did everything perfectly at my lesson today. And Thunderbolt knows how to jump. We are ready. I know it."

"Then don't listen to Clint," Darcy said. "What does he know? He's not up there in the saddle with you. If you think you're ready, then you are."

Allie stared at Darcy as if she had gone crazy. "What do you mean? You think Stephanie should just ignore her instructor?"

"Well, she doesn't have much time left before the Christmas show," Darcy pointed out. "If Clint won't let her jump, then she just has to teach herself."

"You're absolutely right," Stephanie cried.

"That's what I'm going to do." She handed Thunderbolt's reins to Darcy. "Hold him for a minute."

"Steph, I don't think this is a good idea," Allie called.

Stephanie ignored her. She ran across the ring and picked up one of the poles Clint had used in the cavalletti. She pulled it over to one of the gates that were scattered around the ring. She had watched Hannah's lessons often enough to know how the jumps were set up.

After a moment's consideration she decided to set the pole on the second rung—about a foot and a half off the ground.

"What are you doing?" Allie demanded when Stephanie went to collect Thunderbolt.

"Jumping," Stephanie said. She swung into the saddle and carefully looped the reins through her fingers.

"Okay, boy, let's take it slow," Stephanie whispered to Thunderbolt. "Remember, I've never done this before."

Stephanie gave her friends a confident smile. But her heart pounded painfully—and not just because she was breaking the rules. Now that she was actually going to jump, she felt nervous.

Allie had her arms crossed over her chest. She looked worried.

Darcy gave Stephanie a thumbs-up.

"Don't worry, Allie," Stephanie said. "It's only a foot and a half off the ground."

She squeezed Thunderbolt with her knees. The horse started at an easy trot. *I can do this,* Stephanie thought. She took a deep breath. *I know how to trot, and I know how to lift myself up when Thunderbolt jumps.*

Suddenly Thunderbolt gave a little whinny. He had seen the jump ahead of him. He sped up to a gallop.

Don't go so fast! Stephanie was in a panic. She didn't know how to gallop!

Should she try to stop him? Or were they too close to the jump?

The pole loomed up in front of her. It looked much higher than the cavalletti ever had.

Thunderbolt galloped toward the jump, his hooves pounding the dirt. It was too late to stop him from taking the jump.

Please don't let me fall, Stephanie thought.

She felt Thunderbolt's muscles bunch as he prepared to jump. Stephanie closed her eyes and clung to the reins.

Thunderbolt jumped.

CHAPTER
10

♦ ◄ ◆ ♦

Thunderbolt's powerful shoulders rose up. Stephanie opened her eyes and saw that she was in midair.

Wind rushed by her face as Thunderbolt stretched his legs forward over the jump. There was a small bump, and then they were on the ground again, trotting forward.

Stephanie took a deep breath—and burst out laughing. "That was great!" she cried. "Thunderbolt, that was so much fun!"

Being in the air felt like flying!

"Thunderbolt, you're such a good horse," Stephanie told him. "You knew exactly what to do, didn't you?"

Thunderbolt whinnied.

"Steph?" Allie called. "Are you okay?"

"I'm fine!" Stephanie answered, turning Thunderbolt toward the stables. "I'm great! That was amazing!"

Then she saw Clint striding toward her. His face was bright red and his mouth was clenched into a angry frown.

"What do you think you're doing?" Clint hollered so loudly that Thunderbolt laid back his ears.

Uh-oh, Stephanie thought. *Now I'm in trouble.* "I was just—"

"Don't make excuses," Clint interrupted. "I saw exactly what you did. Get down!"

Stephanie climbed out of the saddle, shaking a little. But she forced herself to meet Clint's angry gaze.

"Why do you think I told you not to ride without me?" Clint demanded. "Because I'm mean? Or stupid?"

Stephanie silently shook her head.

"No!" Clint said. "It's because you're not ready. Not ready—as in you could hurt yourself jumping. Or hurt your horse."

"But I'm fine," Stephanie said. "And so is Thunderbolt. Nothing happened."

"Because you were lucky!" Clint yelled.

"But I did manage to take the jump." Stephanie tried to keep her voice from shaking.

Clint stared at her. Slowly his expression grew

a little softer. She knew he was still angry, but he seemed to be thinking about what she said.

"I should never give you another lesson," Clint said finally. "I should tell Cora to kick you out of here."

Stephanie gasped. "Please don't do that," she begged. "I want to learn to jump more than anything."

"I'm beginning to get that idea."

"I'm sorry I jumped without your permission," Stephanie cried. "I know it was a really stupid thing to do. But I want to jump so much, and we had such a good lesson with the cavalletti. . . . I just had to find out what it felt like to take a real jump."

Clint sighed. "Do you promise never to do that again?"

"Promise!"

"Okay," Clint decided. "Then I'll see you on Thursday."

"Thursday?" Stephanie repeated. "But that's three days away! Couldn't we have a lesson tomorrow? My muscles aren't sore. I don't need a break."

"*I* do." Clint's voice was firm. "I'll see you on Thursday."

"Okay," Stephanie answered.

Allie and Darcy came rushing over as Clint disappeared into the stables. "Steph!" Allie cried. "That was awful!"

"Yeah, Clint was really mad," Darcy put in. "What are you going to do if he won't give you a lesson until Thursday?"

"I guess I'm lucky Clint is still willing to give me lessons at all," Stephanie replied. "I'll just have to do a lot of real jumping on Thursday. Then I can audition for Cora on Friday. And join the intermediate jumping class in the show on Saturday."

"Steph, come look at this!" Michelle called from the stairs as soon as Stephanie got home.

"Not now, Michelle. I have to start my laundry," Stephanie called back.

Michelle stuck her lower lip out. "But I want to show you something important."

Stephanie knew Michelle wouldn't leave her alone until she looked at whatever was so important. She sighed and followed her little sister up to their bedroom.

Michelle broke into a grin as she carefully closed the door behind Stephanie. "I got Becky a present!" Michelle announced.

Stephanie plopped down into her desk chair. "Really? What?"

"I'll show you!" Michelle crawled halfway under her bed. She rummaged around for a few minutes—and then backed out, lugging a bag from the stationery shop.

"What is it?" Stephanie asked.

Michelle sat back on her heels and opened the bag. "The most perfect present! Joey gave me the idea—Joey took me to the mall." Michelle glanced up at Stephanie. "I hope you don't mind that I went shopping with Joey, but he was going anyway and I wasn't doing anything. . . . "

"No problem," Stephanie said. Actually she felt kind of relieved—it was one less thing to deal with before Saturday. "So what did you get?"

"Well, remember Becky's shoe box of riding pictures and ribbons and stuff?" Michelle asked.

"Yeah."

"I got her a photo album to put it all in."

Stephanie groaned. *Oh, no!* she thought. *Michelle took my perfect idea. Now what am I going to get Becky?*

"Wasn't that a great idea?" Michelle asked again.

"Yes," Stephanie replied. "It sure *was*."

CHAPTER
11

◆ ◂ ◆ ◆

"How about this for Becky's birthday present?"
Allie asked on Wednesday afternoon. She held up
a neon-pink apron with bright yellow football play-
ers appliquéd on it.

"Maybe," Stephanie said. "It's nice."

Allie burst out laughing.

"Stephanie, are you okay?" Darcy asked.

"Sure. Why?"

"Because you're staring off into space," Darcy
explained.

"Plus, you said you might buy this apron," Allie
added. "And it's hideous!"

Stephanie glanced at the apron again. Allie was
right—it was the ugliest apron she'd ever seen. Besides, Becky didn't even like to cook that much.

She sighed. They had been in the mall for over an hour, and she still hadn't found a good present.

"Sorry, guys. I was just thinking I should be at the stables," Stephanie explained. "The riding show is in three days! I really can't afford to take a day off. I absolutely have to audition for Cora by tomorrow. Friday, at the latest."

"Steph, why don't you just give up?" Allie asked. "There's no way you're going to get into that class before Saturday."

"Yes, I am," Stephanie insisted. "I have no choice. Come on, let's try another store." She walked out into the mall without waiting for Allie's answer.

She felt a little angry. *Allie shouldn't be telling me to give up,* she thought. *She's my best friend—she should be supportive.*

Darcy and Allie hurried after Stephanie. "Hannah's really sweet," Allie said. "Just tell her you made a mistake. I'm sure she'd understand."

"And if she doesn't, who needs her?" Darcy put in. "You already have two terrific friends."

Stephanie couldn't help but smile. "Listen, you guys—I know you're trying to help. But I don't want to talk about this anymore. So why don't you just help me find a present for Becky?"

Allie sighed. "All right."

"Let's shop," Darcy agreed.

The three girls wandered into a department

store. The first display they saw was filled with picture frames.

"Look at this!" Darcy exclaimed. The frame had plastic rattles glued around the edge. "It's perfect for a baby photo!"

"It's nice," Stephanie said. "But Jesse and Becky already have loads of framed photos of the twins."

Suddenly Allie snatched a frame off the table. "You're going to love this!" she squealed. She turned the frame around so Stephanie could see it. "Ta-da!"

Stephanie gasped. "That is so great!" she cried. She took the frame from Allie and studied it. It was a large wooden frame covered with hand-painted horses of all different breeds.

"That one on the right looks just like Thunderbolt," Stephanie said.

"And look—here's a horse jumping over a fence," Darcy pointed out.

"I'm definitely going to get this," Stephanie decided. "Becky will love it as much as I do. Now I just have to figure out what picture to put in it."

"We're going to play follow the leader all the way back to the stable," Cora announced at the end of Stephanie's dressage class on Thursday. "When I gallop, you gallop. If I drop back into a trot, you do the same thing. Got it?"

"Got it," Stephanie said.

"Got it!" the other girls echoed.

"Yaa!" Cora cried to Stargazer. They took off across the pasture at a spirited gallop.

Janie grinned and took off after Cora. Lily followed behind her. Stephanie dug her heels into Thunderbolt's sides, and he broke into a gallop. Her ponytail flew out behind her as they sped across the grass.

This should be so much fun, she thought. *But I can't stop worrying about the Christmas show.* She absolutely had to convince Cora to let her into that class. She had to talk to her today.

When they got back to the stables, the other girls were all giggling. "That was a fun game!" Janie told Cora.

Cora nodded, her eyes shining. "Great class, guys."

Stephanie dismounted. She walked over to Cora, who had slid off Stargazer's back.

"Hi, Stephanie!" Cora said. "Did you enjoy the class today?"

"Um, yeah," Stephanie said. "But I was wondering . . . do you think I'm ready to move out of the beginners' class yet?"

Cora looked surprised. "Well, no. Not yet."

Stephanie quickly ducked her head so Cora wouldn't see how disappointed she was. "I guess nobody thinks I'm ready."

"What do you mean?" Cora asked.

"Well, I've been taking private jumping lessons with Clint," Stephanie told her.

Cora nodded. "Clint told me—he says you seem like a natural."

"Then why won't he let me take any real jumps?" Stephanie cried. "He keeps saying I'm not ready."

"Well, Stephanie, you *are* only a beginner," Cora pointed out. "And we're bending stable rules a little to allow your private lessons with Clint. So I'm afraid you just have to let him decide when you're ready to jump."

"But I am ready. I know it," Stephanie insisted. "And I'm positive that Thunderbolt is ready to jump."

"Thunderbolt is *always* ready to jump," Cora said, giving the horse an affectionate pat. "But why are you in such a rush to jump?"

"I—I don't know," Stephanie stammered. "It's just fun. I mean, it looks like fun." *And I only have two days to convince you to let me jump in the show and save myself from total embarrassment*, she added silently.

"Well, don't worry," Cora said. "Clint will probably let you try some low jumps in a few weeks. Then, when our next term starts, you can join a jumping class."

Stephanie's eyes flew open wide. "A few *weeks*?"

"Sure—if you're ready," Cora said. She turned

to the other girls. "Okay, everybody. Let's get these horses inside."

"I have a private lesson with Clint now," Stephanie told her. "Is it okay if I just keep Thunderbolt saddled up?"

"Sure thing," Cora said. "And don't be too discouraged. It takes a long time to learn how to jump."

"Thanks," Stephanie said. *But I have only two days,* she thought.

Stephanie led Thunderbolt over to the fence and dismounted. She started to move up Thunderbolt's stirrups into jumping position.

"Hey, Steph!"

Stephanie glanced up from the stirrup. Allie stood behind the fence, looking relieved. "I'm glad I found you," she said.

"What's up?" Stephanie asked.

"My mom is stuck in a meeting. She can't pick me up," Allie replied, rolling her eyes. "Is it okay if I get a ride with you?"

"Sure," Stephanie said. "But it's going to be a few hours—I have my lesson with Clint and then I have some mucking to do."

Allie shrugged. "I don't mind watching."

"Actually, when it comes to mucking, you could help," Stephanie said.

Allie made a face. "I don't mind *watching*," she repeated.

Clint opened the fence at the far end of the ring and let himself in.

"Here comes Clint," Stephanie told Allie in a low voice. "I hope today is the big day. I hope he lets me jump!"

"Do you think he will?" Allie asked.

Stephanie bit her lip. "I don't know," she admitted. "Cora says I'm still not ready. But if Clint lets me jump today, I'll be able to show Cora that she's wrong."

"Ready for your lesson?" Clint asked as he walked up.

"Absolutely," Stephanie said.

"Good!" Clint patted Thunderbolt's side. "I have a lot planned for you today."

Stephanie almost fainted with relief. *A lot planned*, she repeated to herself. *That must mean he's going to let me jump!*

"Thank you! Thank you!" Stephanie cried. "You're the best teacher in the whole wide world!"

Clint's eyes grew wide. "Thanks—but what did I do?"

"You're going to let me jump!"

Allie cringed and shook her head at Stephanie.

"Aren't you?" Stephanie asked. "I mean, isn't that what you have planned?"

"No!" Clint's expression grew angry. "Stephanie, let's not go over this again. You're not ready to jump. Until you are, no jumping!"

Stephanie nodded wordlessly. She blinked back the tears that were welling up in her eyes.

"I thought you understood that after what happened last time," Clint said. "If you want to learn how to jump, you do it the way I tell you. Got it?"

"Yes," Stephanie whispered.

Clint stared at her for another few seconds. "Good. I'll set up the cavalletti."

"Okay," Stephanie mumbled.

Clint stalked off toward the poles. Allie put a hand on Stephanie's shoulder. "Are you all right?"

Stephanie took a shaky breath. "Fine," she said. "Except now there's no way I can get into Cora's class."

"Oh, Steph . . . " Allie's green eyes were worried.

"Let's go!" Clint called. "Take it at a walk to warm up."

"Don't worry, Steph," Allie said. "We'll figure something out."

"Thanks." Stephanie swung herself into the saddle. She walked Thunderbolt through the cavalletti. But she barely even noticed the horse's movements. She was busy trying to think of a way—any way—she could compete with the intermediate jumping class on Saturday.

Maybe I can enter without Cora's permission, Stephanie thought as she trotted Thunderbolt through the cavalletti course.

"Try it once more at a trot, Steph," Clint called

97

when she had finished her second course. "And concentrate."

I am concentrating—on something more important than these dumb cavalletti, Stephanie thought.

She rode Thunderbolt back to the beginning and started the course again.

The intermediate class jumps three-foot gates, Stephanie thought as she rode. That was twice as high as the pole she jumped the other day. But maybe if she learned how to make a jump like that, Cora would realize that she belonged in the intermediate class.

Thunderbolt finished the course again.

"One more time!" Clint called.

Stephanie automatically rode back to the start.

The one-and-a-half-foot jump was a little scary at first, Stephanie remembered. *I bet three feet would be much worse*, she thought now. *But I have to do it. I have no choice. I'm out of time!*

"Concentrate!" Clint told her.

Stephanie nodded absently. *Okay*, she thought. *So I'm going to teach myself how to take a three-foot jump. And then I'll show Cora that I'm already as good as an intermediate student.* But that meant she had only today to learn the three-foot jump.

"Come on, Steph!" Clint called. "Pay attention."

Clint definitely won't help me, Stephanie thought. *So I'll just have to do it on my own.*

"Okay, Thunderbolt," she said as they began the

cavalletti course again. "You and I are going to jump three feet today."

She aimed the beautiful horse at the cavalletti and concentrated on lifting herself out of her seat as he stepped over the poles. Suddenly Stephanie couldn't wait for her lesson with Clint to end.

Finally Clint glanced at his watch and gave Stephanie a satisfied smile. "I guess we'd better wrap it up," he told her. "Good work today. You're progressing very quickly."

"Thanks," Stephanie said. "Well . . . I guess I'd better get to work on my mucking!"

"Great," Clint said. "I'll be in the office for a while if you need me."

Allie came forward as Stephanie dismounted. "That was cool! You're getting good at jumping those little crisscrossed things."

Stephanie glanced at Clint. He was just disappearing around the side of the stables. "Well, if you think *that* was cool, just wait until you see what's next!"

Allie's eyes widened. "What?"

"I'm going to jump a three-foot jump," Stephanie announced.

"What?" Allie cried. "Are you crazy?"

"No," Stephanie said as she tied Thunderbolt to the fence. "I have a plan."

"Steph, don't be stupid!" Allie's voice sounded worried. "Clint said you weren't ready. And last time you jumped, he almost kicked you out of the stables!"

"I know," Stephanie said. "But Clint is wrong— I *am* ready. The intermediate class does three-foot-high jumps. I'll teach myself to jump that high, then I'll show Clint and Cora. They'll realize they were wrong to hold me back."

"This is not worth it, Steph," Allie insisted. "So what if you're a little embarrassed in front of Hannah? It was all a big misunderstanding."

Allie's voice died off as Stephanie strode toward the jump.

She pulled the poles out of their crisscrossed bracket and set one up on the three-foot mark. The pole hit her just below chest-high. Stephanie's heart started to thud when she saw just how far off the ground the pole was. Maybe Allie was right. Maybe this was a bad idea.

Calm down, she commanded herself. *This isn't much higher than the first jump I did. And that was a blast! So this will be even more fun.*

Allie's face was pale when Stephanie headed back to the fence. "Last time you tried this, you almost fell." She waved a shaky finger at the jump. "And that thing is even taller than it was before."

"Don't worry." Stephanie swung up into Thunderbolt's saddle. "Now I know how to hold myself out of the saddle when I jump. That's what Clint has been teaching me with the cavalletti."

"Steph, it's against the rules to ride without an instructor," Allie pointed out. "You could get in major trouble."

"I know. But it's just this once," Stephanie promised. "As soon as I show Cora I belong in her other class, I'll never break the rules again."

She turned Thunderbolt away from Allie's worried face. "Let's go, boy," she told the horse. "Let's jump!"

Stephanie dug her heels into his sides, and Thunderbolt began to gallop. It felt much faster than it had earlier in the afternoon, when Cora was nearby.

When Stephanie turned Thunderbolt toward the jump, she was amazed by how high it looked.

Too high.

Stephanie felt cold all over. *I don't know how to do this,* she suddenly realized. *I won't be able to stay in the saddle if Thunderbolt jumps that high.*

I'm not ready!

The jump grew closer and closer.

I've got to stop, Stephanie thought. *Clint was right.*

She pulled on Thunderbolt's reins. "Whoa, boy," she called. But her voice was carried away in the wind.

Thunderbolt galloped faster and faster. The jump loomed up in front of them.

"Stop!" Stephanie yelled. She yanked harder on the reins.

Thunderbolt galloped on.

I'm totally out of control, Stephanie thought in a panic. *I can't stop him!*

The pole was right in front of them.

Thunderbolt barreled toward the jump at a frightening speed. As his front legs left the ground, he seemed to go even faster. His neck reared up-ward—and slammed right into Stephanie's face. She spat out a mouthful of mane.

The horse's powerful legs stretched across the pole. Stephanie tried to lean forward like Clint had taught her on the cavalletti. But she found herself thrown backward in the saddle instead.

The reins slipped from her fingers.

I'm going to fall! Stephanie thought in horror.

CHAPTER
12

♦ ◄ ◢ ♦

At the last second Stephanie threw herself toward Thunderbolt's head and grasped a handful of mane. She held on tight as they flew through the air.

Thunderbolt cleared the jump and plummeted toward the ground on the other side. Stephanie's stomach lurched.

Thunderbolt's front legs hit the ground.

Stephanie whacked into his back with enough force to knock the wind out of her. As she struggled to breathe, she heard a loud clanking noise. Thunderbolt's rear legs must have hit the pole.

Stephanie heard Allie scream.

But she didn't have time to worry about the pole. Thunderbolt's back legs hit the ground. And then he stumbled.

Oh, no! We're going to crash! Stephanie thought. She closed her eyes. But Thunderbolt quickly caught his balance.

Stephanie pulled herself back into the saddle and hauled on the reins. "Whoa!"

Thunderbolt quickly slowed to a stop.

Allie came running across the ring. "Are you okay?"

"I—" Stephanie glanced down at herself. "I think so. . . ." But her heart pounded wildly. Her hands shook as she dismounted.

Even Thunderbolt seemed spooked. His eyes showed white, and his sides were covered with a thin coat of sweat.

"That was so scary! Thunderbolt hit the pole!" Allie cried, throwing her arms around Stephanie. "Are you sure you're all right?"

"I'm okay," Stephanie said. "But I can't believe I didn't just kill myself. I almost fell!" She stroked Thunderbolt's neck to calm him down.

"I know." Allie shivered. "When Thunderbolt hit the pole, I thought you were *both* going to fall." Suddenly Allie clapped a hand over her mouth. "Oh, no! I forgot that I screamed—I hope Clint didn't hear me."

The girls turned toward the stable. Stephanie expected to see Clint or Cora or one of the other instructors striding toward her. But the only people around were a middle-aged couple. They looked like tourists. They were taking photographs—and not paying any attention to Stephanie and Allie.

"Nobody's coming," Allie said with relief.

"I think we're safe," Stephanie agreed.

"You're not going to jump again, are you?" Allie asked.

"No way!" Stephanie shook her head firmly. "Clint was right—I'm not ready to jump. What I just did was really stupid."

Allie grinned. "I am *so* glad to hear you say that!"

Stephanie took a deep breath. She could feel the pounding of her heart start to slow down. "Come on—let's get the mucking done and go home."

Stephanie took Thunderbolt's reins and started to lead him to the stable. He resisted at first. Then he gave a soft huff and began to follow Stephanie.

"What are you going to do about Hannah?" Allie asked.

Stephanie frowned. She had been so frightened by the jump that she'd forgotten all about Hannah.

"I—I guess I'll have to tell her the truth some-how," she said slowly. "And I'll call Sari and tell her not to print that story about me in *The Scribe*."

Stephanie expected Allie to be happy. After all, she had been trying to convince Stephanie to confess ever since she came up with her crazy plan. But Allie's forehead was wrinkled with worry. "Stephanie—stop!" she ordered.

"Huh? What's wrong?" Stephanie asked.

"Thunderbolt!" Allie exclaimed. "He's limping! I think he's hurt."

Stephanie's breath caught in her throat. "Limping? He can't be!"

Allie's green eyes were wide with fear. "He must have hurt himself on the jump."

"Oh, no," Stephanie cried. "It's all my fault!"

"Maybe . . . maybe I just imagined it," Allie said.

Stephanie handed Allie the reins. "Lead him toward the stable," she demanded. "I want to see for myself."

Allie pulled gently on the reins. Thunderbolt obediently started to follow. But as he walked, he set his left hind hoof on the ground for only a brief moment. He didn't put any weight on it.

"Stop!" Stephanie called in alarm.

Allie immediately stopped. Stephanie studied the horse. Thunderbolt held his left hind leg so that his hoof was a few inches off the ground.

"You're right," Stephanie told Allie. Tears welled up in her eyes. "He's hurt."

"I think that's the leg he hit on the pole." Allie's voice sounded frightened. "What are we going to do?"

"I don't know," Stephanie admitted.

Allie swallowed hard. "Don't—um, don't they destroy horses with broken legs?"

Stephanie gasped. "No! At least, I hope not. . . ."

Quickly, she stooped and ran her hand down Thunderbolt's leg. "But I don't think his leg is broken."

"What's wrong, then?" Allie asked.

Stephanie groaned in frustration. "I don't know!"

She blinked back her tears. *I did something completely stupid and selfish*, she thought. *And now I hurt Thunderbolt.*

Stephanie took a deep breath and reached for the reins. She pulled on them as gently as possible. "Come on, boy," she said.

"What are you doing?" Allie asked, walking next to her.

"I'm going to put Thunderbolt in his box," Stephanie said. "And then I'm going to get help."

"From Clint?"

"Right."

"But won't he be mad?" Allie asked. "He might kick you out of the stables."

"I don't care what happens to me," Stephanie said. "We've got to get help for Thunderbolt."

Allie nodded.

Getting Thunderbolt back into the stables took forever. Stephanie let the horse walk as slowly as he wanted. She didn't want to risk hurting him any more.

"Will you stay with him?" Stephanie asked

when Thunderbolt was settled in his box. "I'll go to the office for Clint."

"Okay." Allie laid a hand on Thunderbolt's soft shoulder. "Good boy," she crooned.

Stephanie quickly let herself out of the box. She ran toward the office and threw open the door.

A young woman stood behind the counter, vacuuming. "Boots!" she barked at Stephanie.

"What?"

The woman pointed at Stephanie's muddy boots. "Please take your boots off before you come in here," she said.

"Oh—sorry," Stephanie said. "But I was looking for Clint."

"He went home."

"Already?"

"It's after six," the cleaning woman said.

"It is?" *Dad is supposed to pick me up at six,* Stephanie realized. She hadn't known it was so late. "It's really important. Are any of the other instructors around?"

"Not after six," the cleaning woman replied. "Now, if you don't mind . . ." She looked again at Stephanie's boots.

"Right. Sorry," Stephanie said.

What am I going to do now? Stephanie's mind was going a million miles a second as she made her way back to the stables. *Dad's probably waiting for me already. But Thunderbolt needs help.*

"What did Clint say?" Allie asked as soon as Stephanie got back to Thunderbolt's box.

"He's gone. Everyone's gone."

"Oh, no!" Allie exclaimed. "What are we going to do?"

Stephanie quickly unstrapped Thunderbolt's saddle and slipped it off. "Brush him down. He might get a cold if we don't."

Allie quickly grabbed a brush and gingerly started to brush Thunderbolt's legs.

"You know, Steph, I don't see anything wrong with Thunderbolt's leg," Allie said. "If he broke it, don't you think it would swell up?"

"Probably," Stephanie said. "But I'm really not sure."

Suddenly Allie stopped brushing and stood up. "That sounds like your father's horn!"

Stephanie listened for a second. She heard a distant *beep, beep.*

"You're right—that's him," Stephanie agreed.

"We'd better go," Allie said.

"What about the mucking-out?" Stephanie asked.

Allie shrugged helplessly. "Maybe Clint won't notice."

Stephanie snorted. "I doubt that! But, Allie, what are we going to do about Thunderbolt?"

They both looked at the horse. He still held his

hoof up off the ground. But he pulled a mouthful of hay out of the rack and calmly began chewing.

Allie watched him thoughtfully. "Something is definitely making him limp," she said. "But he doesn't look as if he's in pain. And when I touch his leg, it doesn't seem to hurt. I think he'll be okay overnight."

"I don't want to leave him," Stephanie said.

"I know," Allie replied. "But what else can we do?"

"I don't know," Stephanie said for what felt like the hundredth time. "I don't have Clint's number at home. Or Cora's."

Beep! Beep! The honking was louder now.

"Come on, Steph," Allie said in her quiet voice. "Let's go. You know your dad is a total worrywart. He's probably ready to call the police about now. And Thunderbolt obviously isn't in pain."

"You're right." Stephanie hesitated another moment. Then she reached forward and kissed Thunderbolt's muzzle. "Don't worry," she told the horse softly. "I'll be back soon."

I just hope you'll be okay, she added to herself.

CHAPTER
13

◆ ◂ ◾ ◆

"Hi, Steph," Allie said over the phone later that evening. "It's me."

"And me," Darcy added.

Allie had gotten three-way calling for Christmas a few years before. It came in handy. Especially when Stephanie, Allie, and Darcy needed to put all three of their heads together.

"Hi, you guys." Stephanie flopped down on the living room couch with a heavy sigh.

"Allie just told me what happened," Darcy said. "Are you okay, Steph?"

"Not really," Stephanie admitted. "I keep wondering how I could have done something so awful."

"Come on," Darcy said. "You didn't do anything *that* bad."

"Yes, I did," Stephanie insisted. "I was so impatient that I didn't pay attention to Clint. And because of me, Thunderbolt is hurt!"

"Don't be so hard on yourself," Allie said. "Thunderbolt seemed fine when we left."

"This is all my fault," Stephanie said. "If I hadn't been too chicken to tell Hannah the truth, none of this would have happened."

"What are you going to tell her?" Darcy asked.

"I don't know," Stephanie said. "It doesn't seem so important anymore. I mean, all I cared about was learning how to jump—fast. I didn't even think about learning to do it the right way."

"Well, maybe not," Allie admitted. "But there's nothing you can do about it now."

"I know," Stephanie said. "I wish I could rewind my life back to this afternoon. If I had it to do over, I'd definitely listen to Clint and not jump."

"But you can't do that," Allie pointed out.

"I know," Stephanie said again. "So I'm going to do the next best thing. I'm going to go to the stables first thing in the morning. Then I'll tell Clint exactly what happened."

"Do you think you'll get in trouble?" Darcy asked.

"Definitely," Stephanie said with a sigh. "I'll probably get kicked out of the stables. But I don't care. The most important thing is making sure Thunderbolt is totally healthy."

"What time does the stable open?" Darcy asked.

"Super early," Stephanie replied. "I think there's a class for adults that starts at seven o'clock. And I'll be there."

At exactly 2:56 that morning, Stephanie turned over on her left side. She squeezed her eyes shut. *Go to sleep!* she ordered herself.

After what seemed like an hour, Stephanie flopped onto her right side. The clock on her bedside table read 2:57.

In the next bed Michelle's breathing was soft and deep. Obviously *she* wasn't having trouble sleeping.

Stephanie groaned. *I'm never going to fall asleep,* she thought.

Shifting onto her back, Stephanie decided to count sheep. She closed her eyes. She imagined identical fluffy white sheep bounding over a wooden fence. One, she counted silently. Two. Three.

When Stephanie got to four, the fluffy white sheep turned into horses. Black horses with a white star and intelligent brown eyes—like Thunderbolt.

And each time Thunderbolt jumped over the fence, he whacked his hind leg on the top rung. Hard!

Stephanie's eyes filled with tears. What if Thunderbolt *wasn't* all right? What if he really had hurt his leg? *I'm so sorry, Thunderbolt,* she thought. *But I'm going to set things right—if this night ever ends. . . .*

At six-thirty the next morning Stephanie quietly sat up in bed. It was the perfect time for her to leave the house without anyone noticing. Her father and Becky had left for work about half an hour earlier. The rest of the family wasn't awake yet.

I'm coming, Thunderbolt, Stephanie thought. She tiptoed across the room and opened the closet as quietly as possible. Silently Stephanie slipped off her pajamas. She pulled on a pair of jeans and a sweatshirt and crept down into the kitchen.

Stephanie quickly wrote a note explaining where she was going. She left it on the kitchen counter near the coffeemaker. *Joey will definitely find that first thing,* Stephanie thought. *He never does anything in the morning before he has a cup of coffee.*

Pulling on her backpack, she slipped out the kitchen door. A few minutes later she caught a nearly empty bus toward the stables. When the bus stopped at the park, she eagerly jumped out and ran toward the stables. The place was still closed up tight. But when Stephanie tried the stable door, it was unlocked.

Her stomach did a flip-flop when she heard voices coming from the office. *Someone's here al-*

ready, Stephanie thought. *Should I go tell them about Thunderbolt?*

A soft neigh came from the stables.

I'll just go see how Thunderbolt's doing first, she decided. She crept down the aisle between the rows of boxes and stopped in front of Thunderbolt.

The horse looked up at Stephanie with his soft brown eyes. Then he lowered his muzzle and gave a soft snort in greeting.

"I know you're surprised to see me so early in the morning," Stephanie whispered. "But I had to come see how your leg is."

Slipping into the box, Stephanie moved to Thunderbolt's backside. Her heart sank when she saw that he still held his hoof off the ground.

Stephanie leaned her head against Thunderbolt's warm flank. "Oh, Thunderbolt. What did I do to you?"

Stephanie was startled by a noise behind her. She spun around to see Clint standing at the door to Thunderbolt's box. He looked surprised to see her.

"Stephanie! What are you doing here?" Clint asked. "Shouldn't you be in school?"

Stephanie swallowed hard. Her throat felt dry. *I'm about to get into big big trouble*, she thought.

"Clint, I have something to tell you," Stephanie said. "Something bad."

CHAPTER
14

◆ ◀ ◢ ◆

"I—" Stephanie glanced down at Thunderbolt's leg to summon up her courage. "I came to talk to you about Thunderbolt."

Clint's forehead wrinkled in confusion. Clearly he had no idea what she was talking about. "What about Thunderbolt?" he demanded.

"His leg might be hurt," Stephanie said. "What I mean is—I hurt his leg yesterday."

"What?" Clint cried. "How?"

Stephanie tried to ignore the painful way her heart was pounding. "I jumped him over a three-foot jump yesterday after you left. He hit his leg on the pole."

For an awful moment Clint just stared at Stephanie. She forced herself to meet his eyes.

Thunderbolt seemed to sense that something

was wrong. He nudged Stephanie's shoulder with his nose.

"How could you do that?" Clint finally exploded. "I told you over and over that you weren't ready."

Tears flooded Stephanie's eyes. "I know," she whispered.

"You could have killed yourself," Clint cried. "And I'm not kidding."

"I'm fine," Stephanie said. "It's Thunderbolt that's hurt. Will you please look at him?"

"And how could you have put this poor horse in danger?" Clint muttered as he brushed by Stephanie.

"I don't know," Stephanie admitted. "It was a super stupid thing to do. I never thought Thunderbolt could get hurt."

Clint gently ran his hands the length of Thunderbolt's leg. Thunderbolt swished his tail and ate some hay.

Please don't let it be broken, Stephanie begged silently. *Please don't say that he'll never run again.* "Is it—is it bad?" she asked.

"I don't know." Clint stood up and brushed off his hands. "We'll have to ask the vet," he said.

The vet? *Oh, no!* Stephanie thought. "That sounds serious," she said as she followed Clint out of the box.

"We call a veterinarian whenever something is

wrong with one of the horses," Clint told her. "Horses are very delicate—and very valuable. Now come into the office. I want you to tell Cora what happened."

I have to confess again? Stephanie's stomach lurched at the thought. But she squared her shoulders as she trailed after Clint. Telling Cora what she did wouldn't be fun. But she had gotten herself into this mess. And she had to tell the truth. Thunderbolt deserved that.

"Can you help him?" Stephanie asked.

She stood with Cora and Clint outside Thunderbolt's box. The veterinarian, a gray-haired man with a neat beard, bent to examine Thunderbolt's leg. He ran his hand up and down the leg, squeezing gently. Then he picked up Thunderbolt's hoof. He held it between his knees and tapped on it with a tiny hammer.

"Hmmm," he murmured, his face expressionless.

Hmmm? Stephanie thought in frustration. *Is that a good sign or not?*

"Well?" she burst out. "What do you think?"

The veterinarian dropped Thunderbolt's hoof and gave the horse a sound pat on the rump. "This is no job for a vet," he told Stephanie. He picked up his bag and started to make his way out of the box.

Stephanie grabbed his arm. "What do you mean?" she asked. "Don't go! I'm sure you can help Thunderbolt. Please try."

The vet started to laugh. "Relax," he said, patting Stephanie's hand. "Thunderbolt doesn't need my help. That horse is as healthy as can be."

Stephanie couldn't believe what she was hearing. "But his leg . . ."

"There's nothing wrong with his leg. It's his hoof that's the problem," the vet explained.

"What's wrong?" Cora asked.

"He threw a shoe," the vet answered. "Nothing that a blacksmith couldn't fix in two seconds flat!"

Cora chuckled.

Stephanie almost fainted with happiness. "That's—that's incredible. It's terrific!"

Stephanie rushed into Thunderbolt's box and threw her arms around her horse's neck. "Thunderbolt, you're fine!" she told him. "You just need new shoes!"

The veterinarian smiled. "One shoe, actually."

Clint's tense look relaxed. "I was so angry that I didn't even think to check his shoes," he said. "Thanks, Doc."

"No problem," the vet answered. "See you next time."

Cora turned to face Stephanie. "As for you, young lady." She wagged a finger in Stephanie's face. "I've been thinking about how to punish you."

Stephanie stopped smiling. She had been so relieved about Thunderbolt that she'd forgotten all about being punished. She glanced down at her feet. "Are you going to throw me out of the stables?" she asked in a small voice.

Cora looked thoughtful. "Well, you were completely irresponsible. And you took advantage of Clint's trust. Also, you should know better than to ride without supervision. You could have broken your neck yesterday."

"I know," Stephanie said. "And I could have hurt Thunderbolt."

Clint shook his head. "If you really love riding—"

"I do!" Stephanie interrupted.

"Then you'll spend the time to learn how to do it properly," Clint said. "You can't just start jumping before you know how."

Stephanie nodded. "I know. As soon as I started for the jump, I realized that I should have listened to you. I really wasn't ready. I was being impatient."

"You sure were," Clint agreed. "And that's dangerous when you're learning to ride."

"But I won't do that anymore," Stephanie promised. "That is, if you guys will still let me ride."

Cora gave Stephanie a smile. "I can tell how much you like Thunderbolt. And I'd hate to separate you two. So I guess I won't throw you out."

"Really?" Stephanie cried. "Thanks, Cora! I promise I'll be good."

"Wait a second," Cora said. "You're not off the hook that easily. I won't kick you out, but you are on probation. If you disobey Clint or me even once, that's it."

"I understand," Stephanie said.

"And I want to make sure you realize that riding isn't all glamorous and exciting. You have to do a lot of hard work in order to be a great rider."

"I know that now," Stephanie said.

"Good. But just to make sure you remember, I want you to muck out all of the stables after every lesson you take."

Stephanie looked at Clint and groaned. Not *more* mucking out!

"Thanks for the ride, Clint! And thanks for being so understanding about Thunderbolt."

Clint had offered to drive Stephanie to school so that she wouldn't be late—and get into even more trouble. He pulled his Jeep up in front of the school just as the early buses were arriving.

"No problem," Clint replied. "See you tomorrow."

Tomorrow? For a moment Stephanie didn't

know what Clint was talking about. But then it all came rushing back to her.

The Christmas horse show! She was supposed to jump in front of the entire school. Everyone expected her to win a ribbon for jumping.

Uh-oh, Stephanie thought. *What am I going to do about the horse show?*

CHAPTER
15

◆ ◀ ◆ ◆

As soon as Stephanie reached the pay phones, Darcy grabbed her arm and pulled her aside. Allie stood next to her.

"Did you get to the stables okay?" Allie demanded. "Whose Jeep was that? Did you see Thunderbolt? Is he okay?"

Stephanie laughed at the steady stream of questions. "Thunderbolt's fine," she replied. "He just threw a shoe! And I told Cora and Clint exactly what happened."

Darcy's dark eyes grew worried. "Are you in big trouble?"

Stephanie made a face. "Only medium trouble. I have to muck out the stalls as punishment. But I can still take lessons. And I can still be in the horse show."

Darcy and Allie exchanged concerned glances. "You're still going to try to compete with the intermediates?" Darcy asked.

"No way!" Stephanie cried. "One jump was enough to convince me that I'm totally not ready."

"Was it really that bad?" Darcy asked.

"Yes," Allie put in.

Stephanie nodded. "I was totally clueless. I didn't know how to hold on! It was so scary. Darce—you should have heard Allie scream!"

Allie rolled her eyes. "I didn't scream *that* loud. And besides, it was terrifying. Stephanie was holding on to Thunderbolt by his hair."

"Ugh! Let's not talk about that anymore," Stephanie said. "I'm not jumping again until I'm totally ready."

"Good," Allie said. "Because I don't think I could take any more of you jumping. I'll be happy to see you ride in nice, safe circles tomorrow at the Christmas show."

"Listen, if you guys are too embarrassed to come to the show tomorrow, I'd understand," Stephanie said.

Darcy shook her head. "No way. If you're brave enough to compete with the little kids, we'll be there to cheer you on. Right, Allie?"

"Absolutely," Allie agreed.

"Thanks, you guys," Stephanie said. "You really are the best friends in the world."

"Speaking of friends, what are you going to tell Hannah?" Allie asked.

"I haven't really thought about that yet." Stephanie switched her book bag to the other shoulder.

"Well, think fast," Darcy said. "Here she comes."

Stephanie took a deep breath. *Don't chicken out,* she told herself. Then she turned around.

Hannah hurried down the hall toward her, smiling broadly. Hailey and Nicole were at her side.

"Hi, you guys!" Hannah called out. "I'm so glad we ran into you. My dad told me I could take some friends out for pizza after the horse show. And I want you guys to come. We'll go to Tony's, of course."

"I can't!" Stephanie exclaimed. "It's my aunt's birthday tomorrow. We've spent weeks planning a big surprise party for her. In fact, you're all invited—it's sort of a Christmas party–birthday party combo."

Nicole gave Stephanie a puzzled look. "I think my invitation got lost in the mail," she joked.

"Not exactly," Stephanie stammered. "I, er . . ."

Hannah was watching her curiously.

Stephanie took a deep breath. "The thing is . . . I wasn't sure you'd want to come to the party after the horse show—"

"That's the perfect time to party!" Hannah said.

"Especially if you guys win ribbons," Nicole put in. "It will be a celebration."

This is even harder than I expected, Stephanie thought in frustration. "I'm sure you will win a ribbon, Hannah," she said. "But *I* won't. At least not in intermediate jumping."

Hannah smiled. "Don't be so nervous. You're going to be great."

"But I'm not in intermediate jumping!" Stephanie blurted out. "I'm taking beginning dressage."

Hannah's jaw dropped. "I don't understand," she mumbled.

Get it all out, Stephanie told herself. "Remember the day I first saw you at the stables?" she asked Hannah.

Hannah nodded.

"Well, you asked me if I was in Cora's class," Stephanie said.

"And you said yes," Hannah replied. She sounded annoyed.

"Stephanie *is* taking a class with Cora," Allie put in. "Beginning dressage."

"It wasn't until later that I realized you meant Cora's intermediate jumping class," Stephanie explained. "And then I tried to explain, but you'd already told everyone I knew how to jump. So I decided to learn. . . ."

Stephanie's voice trailed off when she saw Hannah's eyebrows fly up. *She thinks I'm crazy!* Stephanie thought miserably.

"I mean, I did *want* to learn how to jump," she added. "My aunt, Becky, was a show jumper, and I wanted to be one, too. I had no idea that I wouldn't learn to jump in the baby class. I mean, the beginning dressage class. . . . "

I'm babbling, Stephanie realized. *Hannah is definitely never going to talk to me again.*

Darcy gave Stephanie an encouraging smile. "Steph's been taking private lessons with Clint," she explained. "And she almost learned how to jump well enough to compete tomorrow. If she'd had a few more days, she would have definitely won a jumping ribbon."

Hannah burst out laughing. "You can't learn how to jump in a few weeks! I was riding for three years before I made the intermediate class."

"Three *years*?" Stephanie stared at her, astonished. "I thought you were just naturally talented."

Hannah shook her head. "Nobody is *that* talented. Jumping takes forever. You have to learn all the basics before you can make even a one-foot jump!"

"Yeah, I kind of found that out," Stephanie admitted.

"But, Steph, I still don't understand why you didn't tell me the truth," Hannah said.

"I was too embarrassed!" Stephanie exclaimed. "All the other kids in my class are so young." She swallowed hard. "And I thought you wouldn't want to be my friend if you found out I was just a beginner," she added.

Hannah put a hand on Stephanie's shoulder. "I don't care about that!" she said with a laugh. "I'm just glad to have a friend who loves horses as much as I do."

"You're not mad at me?" Stephanie asked.

"Well, I wish you had told me the truth," Hannah admitted. "But I guess I might have done the same thing."

"Well, I want to know one thing," Nicole demanded.

Stephanie's stomach did a nervous flip-flop. "What?"

Nicole put her hands on her hips. "Are we going for pizza at Tony's or to Stephanie's party after the riding show?"

Everyone laughed.

Stephanie looked at Hannah. She felt happier than she had in weeks. "I'd really like you to be at the party," she said.

"Okay," Hannah agreed. "But only if I can take you all out for pizza *next* Saturday."

Stephanie held out a hand. Hannah slapped her five.

"Deal!" they said together.

CHAPTER
16

◆ ◀ ◗ ◆

"Our next competitor in Level One dressage is . . . Stephanie Tanner!"

Stephanie fastened the strap on her helmet. Then she leaned forward and rubbed Thunderbolt's neck. "Let's show them our stuff," she whispered in the horse's ear.

Thunderbolt pranced sideways on his new shoes. *He's definitely ready to compete*, Stephanie thought. *And so am I.*

She glanced around at the riding ring. Temporary bleachers had been set up along one side of the ring. Large wreaths with bright red bows decorated the fence, and all the trees near the stable were strung with Christmas lights.

Four judges were scattered around the edge of the ring, each one wearing a Santa hat.

While Stephanie waited for the signal to begin, she quickly scanned the stands.

Her family took up an entire row near the front. Danny, D.J., and Michelle were clapping loudly. Jesse was whispering something to the twins, who looked excited. Joey fiddled with his new Polaroid camera. Becky studied the riding ring.

Next Stephanie found Darcy and Allie. They sat near the top of the stands with Nicole, Hailey and Anna.

One of the judges rang a bell.

"Come on, boy," Stephanie told Thunderbolt. She dug her heels into his sides, and he walked into the riding ring. She stopped the horse exactly in the middle of the ring and saluted the judges. Then Stephanie walked, trotted, and cantered Thunderbolt around the circles that were marked out in the ring.

So far, so good, Stephanie thought. *All that's left now are the figure eights.* Stephanie steered Thunderbolt toward the turns. They trotted through the marked-out figure eights.

"Almost done," Stephanie told Thunderbolt. She walked him back to the center of the ring. As she saluted the judge again, Stephanie broke into a broad grin. *That felt perfect*, she thought proudly. *Thunderbolt and I are a great team!*

* * *

"A blue ribbon!" Hannah cried, riding up to Stephanie. "That's amazing!"

Stephanie grinned at her new friend. "I know. It's my first ribbon ever—but definitely not my last."

Stephanie glanced around. She and Thunderbolt stood in the winner's circle with all the other girls who had received ribbons. Hannah had two blue ribbons and a red ribbon.

"I told you we would both win," Hannah said. "I can't wait to see Sari's picture of us in *The Scribe.*"

Stephanie nodded. *I don't know what I was so worried about,* she thought. *Hannah understands better than anyone else I know how hard it is to ride. It's terrific to have a friend like her.*

"Smile!" Joey called from the stands.

Stephanie sat up straighter in the saddle and beamed at Joey.

He looked through the viewfinder on his instant camera. "Beautiful!" he exclaimed as he pressed the shutter release.

Stephanie dismounted and led Thunderbolt over to the stands. "Let me see the picture!" she told Joey.

"Me, too!" Darcy said.

Allie joined the others as they watched the picture quickly sharpen into focus.

Stephanie smiled when she saw the image of herself, seated on the gleaming horse. An oversized blue ribbon was pinned to her chest. Thunderbolt wore a wreath of pointsettias around his neck.

"Hey, Joey," she called. "Can I have this?"

"Sure," Joey said with a grin. "Anything for the champ!"

"Open mine next!" Stephanie got up to hand Becky the package she'd tied with a bright red ribbon. Then she joined her friends on the couch.

"What is it?" Hannah whispered to Stephanie.

"You'll see," Stephanie said. *I hope she likes it,* she added to herself.

Becky slipped off the bow and pulled open the paper. She broke into a grin as she took out the picture frame decorated with horses.

"This is beautiful!" Becky held up the frame so that everyone could see the photo Stephanie had placed inside: Joey's picture of her on Thunderbolt, wearing her blue ribbon. All of the guests clapped, but Stephanie's friends were the noisiest.

"Thank you so much!" Becky told Stephanie. "I'll treasure this always."

Stephanie grinned back. "Thank you again for the riding lessons." She threw a look at all of her friends. "It was one gift I'll always remember!"

Darcy rolled her eyes. "We all will!"

Becky lifted her glass of soda. "Let's toast to horseback riding."

"To riding!" Hannah raised her ginger ale.

"To blue ribbons!" Allie suggested.

"And to friends," Stephanie added.

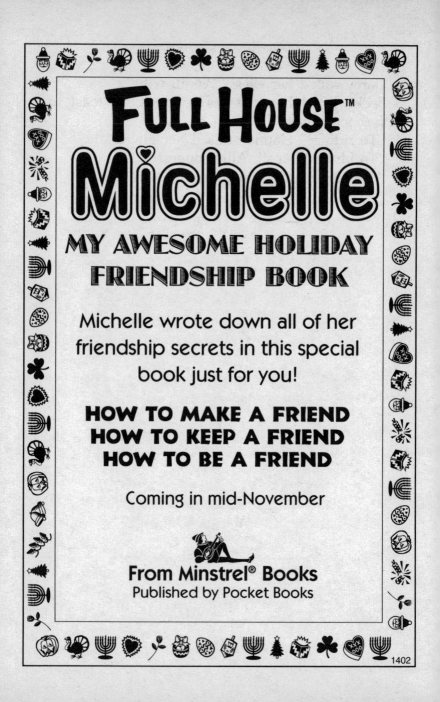

FULL HOUSE™
Michelle

MY AWESOME HOLIDAY FRIENDSHIP BOOK

Michelle wrote down all of her friendship secrets in this special book just for you!

HOW TO MAKE A FRIEND
HOW TO KEEP A FRIEND
HOW TO BE A FRIEND

Coming in mid-November

From Minstrel® Books
Published by Pocket Books

1402

It doesn't matter if you live around the corner...
or around the world...
If you are a fan of Mary-Kate and Ashley Olsen,
you should be a member of

MARY-KATE + ASHLEY'S FUN CLUB™

Here's what you get:
Our Funzine™
An autographed color photo
Two black & white individual photos
A full size color poster
An official **Fun Club**™ membership card
A **Fun Club**™ school folder
Two special **Fun Club**™ surprises
A holiday card
Fun Club™ collectibles catalog
Plus a **Fun Club**™ box to keep everything in

To join Mary-Kate + Ashley's Fun Club™, fill out the form
below and send it along with

U.S. Residents – $17.00
Canadian Residents – $22 U.S. Funds
International Residents – $27 U.S. Funds

MARY-KATE + ASHLEY'S FUN CLUB™
859 HOLLYWOOD WAY, SUITE 275
BURBANK, CA 91505

NAME:_____

ADDRESS:_____

_CITY:_____ STATE:_____ ZIP:_____

PHONE:(____) _____ BIRTHDATE:_____

1242

FULL HOUSE™
Stephanie

PHONE CALL FROM A FLAMINGO	88004-7/$3.99
THE BOY-OH-BOY NEXT DOOR	88121-3/$3.99
TWIN TROUBLES	88290-2/$3.99
HIP HOP TILL YOU DROP	88291-0/$3.99
HERE COMES THE BRAND NEW ME	89858-2/$3.99
THE SECRET'S OUT	89859-0/$3.99
DADDY'S NOT-SO-LITTLE GIRL	89860-4/$3.99
P.S. FRIENDS FOREVER	89861-2/$3.99
GETTING EVEN WITH THE FLAMINGOES	52273-6/$3.99
THE DUDE OF MY DREAMS	52274-4/$3.99
BACK-TO-SCHOOL COOL	52275-2/$3.99
PICTURE ME FAMOUS	52276-0/$3.99
TWO-FOR-ONE CHRISTMAS FUN	53546-3/$3.99
THE BIG FIX-UP MIX-UP	53547-1/$3.99
TEN WAYS TO WRECK A DATE	53548-X/$3.99
WISH UPON A VCR	53549-8/$3.99
DOUBLES OR NOTHING	56841-8/$3.99
SUGAR AND SPICE ADVICE	56842-6/$3.99
NEVER TRUST A FLAMINGO	56843-4/$3.99
THE TRUTH ABOUT BOYS	00361-5/$3.99
CRAZY ABOUT THE FUTURE	00362-3/$3.99
MY SECRET ADMIRER	00363-1/$3.99
BLUE RIBBON CHRISTMAS	00830-7/$3.99

Available from Minstrel® Books Published by Pocket Books